CITY SECRETS

CANTERWOOD CREST

CITY SECRETS

JESSICA BURKHART

ALADDIN M!X

New York London Toronto Sydney

M!X

ALADDIN M!X

Simon & Schuster Children's Publishing Division

1230 Avenue of the Americas, New York, NY 10020

First Aladdin M!X edition July 2010

Text copyright © 2010 by Jessica Burkhart

All rights reserved, including the right of reproduction
in whole or in part in any form.

ALADDIN is a trademark of Simon & Schuster, Inc., and related logo
is a registered trademark of Simon & Schuster, Inc.

ALADDIN M!X and related logo are registered trademarks
of Simon & Schuster, Inc.

For information about special discounts for bulk purchases, please
contact Simon & Schuster Special Sales at 1-866-506-1949
or business@simonandschuster.com.

The Simon & Schuster Speakers Bureau can bring authors to your live event.
For more information or to book an event contact the Simon & Schuster Speakers
Bureau at 1-866-248-3049 or visit our website at www.simonspeakers.com.

Designed by Jessica Handelman

The text of this book was set in Venetian 301 BT.

Manufactured in the United States of America / 1114 OFF

8 10 9 7

Library of Congress Control Number 2010902790

ISBN 978-1-4424-0380-2

ISBN 978-1-4424-0381-9 (eBook)

To the dedicated, smart, funny, and brilliant
reader girlies on Team Canterwood

ACKNOWLEDGMENTS

Huge thank-yous to everyone for helping create this book and supporting it, including Fiona Simpson, Bethany Buck, Mara Anastas, Jessica Handelman, Karin Paprocki, Russell Gordon, Liesa Abrams, Brenna Franzitta, Katherine Devendorf, Dayna Evans, Alyson Heller, Lucille Rettino, Bess Braswell, Venessa Williams, Nicole Russo, and Monica Stevenson.

Thanks so much to the gorgeous, talented models for making this cover so beautiful!

Kate Angelella, you waved your sparkly purple editor wand over my first draft and transformed it into a book. I know, I know, it's hard for you to take a compliment, *but* you are truly a superstar editor and writer who is only going to continue to take over the publishing biz. No doubt. Brainstorming date in your fort soon?

Ross Angelella, the Shake Shack references are all you! ☺

Hugs to all of the readers who allow me to keep doing what I love.

Kate, you intimidate me (in the best possible way!) with your writing and I never stop learning from you—both in business and in life. Our adventures never get any less exciting and I always know we're going to have epic fun when we hang out, b. And, hello, I've got you hooked on watermelon and cotton candy gloss—my goal is to get you to like one of those "complicated" flavors. ☺ LYSSMB. <3

CITY SECRETS

PARK AVENUE
PRINCESS

I PEERED OUT THE TINTED WINDOW OF HEATHER
Fox's Lincoln Town Car and stared up at her building on
Park Avenue in NYC. Twenty-four hours ago I'd *never* imag-
ined I'd be spending fall break with my former arch nemesis.

"Wow," I said, turning to Heather. "You live *here*?"

She flicked her blond hair over her shoulder and rolled
her eyes. "Don't freak out, Silver. This is just the driveway. If you're acting like this now, you might have a stroke
when we get inside."

This was where I'd be staying for Canterwood Crest's
weeklong fall break. Until last night I'd been supposed
to stay with my best friend and roommate, Paige Parker,
but . . . my thoughts stopped short. I didn't want to think
about my fight with Paige.

The driver, in a crisp black suit and red tie, halted the car. His brown hair was streaked with gray and he had been supernice to us on the ride from school. He got out of the car, opened Heather's door, and offered her a hand. I scrambled out after her and she sighed.

"Paul was going to come around to your side next," Heather said. "At least act like you've been to a real city before."

"I have," I said. "I—" I shook my head, not wanting to finish the sentence. The last time I'd been to NYC was when I'd visited Paige last summer. We'd been planning this fall break forever, until . . .

"Sasha!" Heather said, putting a hand on her hip. "Space much?"

"Sorry," I said, directing my gaze back to the building. "Forgot what I was going to say."

But there was no way I could forget. Not the awful fight Paige and I'd had last night at Friday's Homecoming dance. In a flash of images I saw Paige and me standing in the bathroom just off the Canterwood Crest ball-room. Paige had accused me of being jealous that Ryan was her boyfriend because I didn't have one. And I'd lost it. It had been too much after I'd suffered through Homecoming week—forced to do activities with Jacob

(my ex-almost-boyfriend) and Eric (my ex-boyfriend). I'd wanted Paige to be more sensitive about everything. But instead she'd turned on me.

The trunk of the car slammed shut and an attendant came and picked up Heather's and my suitcases, loading them onto a cart.

"C'mon," Heather said. "Our stuff will be upstairs in a sec."

I followed her as a doorman tipped his hat, opening the door to let us inside. "Miss Fox," he said.

"Hi, Allen," Heather said. She smiled at him and we walked into a lobby that looked like something out of a movie set. Nothing looked real.

"You have exactly two seconds to gawk before I shove you back in the car," Heather said to me.

I couldn't help it. The white-and-sandy-colored marble floors gleamed. A security guard monitored people heading for one of the six elevators. The gold elevators looked imposing, and elevator attendants waited to offer assistance if necessary.

A giant stone fireplace, surrounded by crimson high-backed chairs, cast heat across the lobby. Gleaming gold fireplace tools were hung on the hearth. It looked like a spot I'd *never* leave during the winter if I lived here. I'd curl

up with *Misty of Chincoteague*, one of my favorite books, and read for hours.

Placed around the room were coffee tables and end tables—most with neat stacks of magazines, and others with vases of flowers. Potted plants were in the corners of the room. There were a few cream-colored couches where people sat and read books or chatted in quiet tones on their phones.

My gaze traveled upward to the high ceiling and six crystal chandeliers that sparkled. Hundreds of crystals dangled from the chandeliers and reflected bits of light onto the ceiling. The chandeliers alone screamed elegance.

On the opposite side of the elevators, a staircase with a gleaming wooden railing wrapped around the side of the room, over the fireplace, and to what looked like another level of the lobby. I stared down at my jeans and flip-flops—I looked *so* out of place here.

"Enough already," Heather said, grabbing my elbow. "People are going to stare. I *do* live here and have to see my neighbors occasionally when I'm here on break."

"Sorry," I said.

I followed Heather past the security desk. She waved at the guard and he smiled at her.

We waited for the elevator, then stepped inside. The doors closed behind us and I almost fell back against wall when I turned to face the door.

"There's a *TV* in your elevator?" I asked.

Heather smirked. "So easily impressed. It's only going to get better from here, so chill before you pass out or something."

"I'm not going to faint," I muttered.

The elevator doors opened and I held my breath as we stepped into the hallway. The walls were eggshell, and the dark gray carpet had red and gold swirls. Golden accents ran along the top of the walls, near the ceiling, and I half-expected a movie star to emerge from one of the rooms. This looked like a building where celebs would *def* live.

We turned the corner and stopped in front of a dark cherrywood doorway labeled PH1 in gold. Heather pressed four numbers into a keypad, and I wiped my sweaty hands on my jeans. Heather's parents weren't exactly . . . *nice*, and Mr. Fox always made me nervous. He never missed a chance to be intimidating or to make the people around him sweat.

The red light on the keypad turned to a blinking green, and Heather pushed down the door handle. I took

another breath, hoping I'd made the right decision by coming here. But it was too late to go back now. My parents had left for vacation, and there was no way I could—or would—stay with Paige. I was stuck here no matter what.

2

TOO LATE TO CHANGE MY MIND

HEATHER OPENED THE DOOR AND WALKED inside. We stepped into the entryway and the only sound in the penthouse was my flip-flops slapping the marble floor. How many times today was I going to regret my shoe choice?

Heather kicked off her wedge platforms and motioned for me to do the same.

"The maid will put them away," she said. "My mother will freak if you wear shoes in the apartment, FYI. She just got the carpets redone."

I stared at the chandelier hanging from the ceiling, the tables that had gorgeous lamps on them, and the sparkling crystal knobs on the closet doors.

"Heather, you're a half hour late."

Mrs. Fox walked into the room in a black v-neck dress. A diamond tennis bracelet sparkled from her wrist. She shared Heather's blond hair, willowy build, and blue eyes.

"Sorry, Mom," Heather said. "Paul hit traffic."

Someone knocked on the door, and Heather, probably glad for the interruption, turned to open it. It was the doorman with our bags. I grabbed mine and Heather took hers.

"Thank you," we both said. He dipped his head and walked away, shutting the door behind him.

"Traffic?" Mrs. Fox asked.

The roads had been clear—Heather had waited until the last possible minute to leave. And from being inside for just two seconds, I already understood why. We'd been held hostage in the foyer since we'd gotten here.

I had to distract Mrs. Fox from questioning Heather. She'd been nice enough to offer for me to stay with her—it was the least I could do.

"Wow," I said, moving toward a crystal vase filled with orchids. It sat on an end table in the entryway. "That's so beau—"

"Please be careful," Mrs. Fox interrupted. "That's from Tiffany."

I stepped back and stood close to Heather.

Mrs. Fox stared at me as if I were some kind of bug or intruder in her home.

"Heather," she said. "Remember your manners and take Sasha to the guest room. There's no need for everyone to be standing in the doorway. I'll see you both at seven for dinner."

And with that Mrs. Fox turned and disappeared down a side hallway.

Heather sighed. "C'mon," she said. "Your room's this way."

I followed Heather through the foyer and down a long hallway. Framed black-and-white photos of the city lined the walls. It felt like a museum, like an alarm would go off if I accidentally touched something. This was *so* unlike my much shorter hallway at home. Mine was decorated with framed "art" I'd created in kindergarten and time-worn family photos. Here there wasn't one picture of Heather or her parents.

Heather stopped in front of a door and twisted the brass knob. A light scent of violet flowed through the open door and I almost dropped my bag.

"This is *my* room?" I asked. "It has a fireplace!"

Heather smirked. "All of the bedrooms have fireplaces, Silver."

Wow. I had a feeling I was going to be thinking that a lot.

I put my bag on the floor and walked over to the sliding glass door with sheer curtains held back by elegant ties. I looked out at a balcony with two wicker chairs, a small glass table, and pots of flowers that I couldn't even attempt to name.

"Can I—" I asked, stopping when Heather nodded.

Heather stepped in front of me and unlatched the door. She slid it open and walked in front of me onto the balcony. I followed her, gasping at the view of New York City.

"It almost feels like we're in an airplane or helicopter hovering over the city," I said.

Heather nodded. "I still get that feeling too. The view is pretty insane."

I looked out over the tops of the buildings that stretched toward the puffy clouds. I grasped the iron railing and a gentle breeze blew my golden-brown hair back. It felt like I was in another country.

"I might sleep out here," I joked.

Heather rolled her eyes. "Only you would say that. C'mon, let me give you a quick tour, and then you can unpack."

"Okay."

I followed Heather out of my room and we walked a few feet down the hallway. Heather pointed to doors on either side.

"Those are two of the other guest rooms. Mom and Dad's room is at the end of the hallway."

"Three guest rooms," I said. "Wow."

"Get a new word before I shove the 'wow' out of you," Heather said. But she smiled.

"Fine," I said. *"Whoa."*

"Your bathroom's down there," Heather said, pointing to another door.

We turned down another hallway and passed giant bay windows that overlooked Manhattan. I couldn't help thinking how different the view was from here than from Paige's apartment. Paige's fifth-floor apartment had a gorgeous view of Central Park, but it couldn't compare to the stunning view Heather's penthouse offered.

"Let's get a snack," Heather said. We walked down another hallway that felt almost hotel-like and entered the kitchen.

We'd no sooner sat on bar stools at the island in the kitchen than a smiling woman appeared. Her dark hair was pulled back in a bun and she had on black pants and a white long-sleeve dress shirt.

"Welcome home, Heather," she said.

"Thanks, Kay," Heather said. "This is my friend Sasha, from school."

I blinked when Heather said "friend," but recovered. Sometimes it was still hard to even entertain the idea that we were friends now.

"Nice to meet you," I said, smiling at Kay.

"And you," she said. "What can I make you girls?"

"A fruit and cheese plate would be great," Heather said. "Do you have the Havarti cheese that I like?"

Kay nodded. "Sure do. I'll make you girls a plate right now."

Kay got grapes, cantaloupe, honeydew melon, pineapple, and a handful of different cheeses out of the Sub-Zero fridge. The glass cabinets were filled with black plates, mugs, and bowls. Kay opened a cabinet near us and took out two glasses. I gulped a little. At home my favorite "glass" was a sparkly plastic cup with a horseshoe on it that Dad had won for me at the Connecticut State Fair. I'd dropped it a zillion times, and it always bounced off the kitchen floor. If I dropped one of *these* glasses, Mrs. Fox would probably make me become a maid for the week to work it off.

Something buzzed and Heather pulled her phone out of her pocket.

She typed a message and put her phone facedown on the counter.

"I love Julia, but she can be *so* annoying sometimes," Heather said. She grabbed a green grape off the plate that Kay set in front of us. Heather was referring to one her BFFs and one-third of their clique—the Trio.

"What's up?" I asked. Heather and I had a tentative friendship, but I wasn't sure if she'd confide in me about Trio business.

Heather took her time placing a piece of Havarti cheese on a wheat cracker. She took a bite, then looked at me.

"Julia's ticked that you're spending break with me. I mean, it's not like she was going to, anyway—her parents planned a killer trip to Miami—but she's being weird that you and I are spending break together."

"What about Alison?" I asked. "How's she acting?" Alison Robb was Heather's other best friend, and I was much closer to Alison than I was to Julia.

Heather waved her hand. "You know Alison likes you way more than Julia does. You did save them both from Jasmine, but Julia still has this thing with you. Alison thinks it's cool that you're here."

Jasmine King was also on the list of things I didn't want to think about. She'd caused destruction the entire time she'd been at Canterwood, until she'd finally been caught and expelled. I speared a strawberry with my fork.

"At least *one* of them thinks that," I said. "Thanks again for letting me stay here. I really didn't want to stay on campus for a week."

Heather leaned closer to me. "As if I wanted to stay *here* by myself for a week."

She stopped talking and we finished the fruit, crackers, and cheese. I couldn't imagine how difficult summers and holidays were for Heather. Her mom wanted nothing to do with her, and I hadn't even seen Mr. Fox yet. No doubt he'd burst into the room and start questioning Heather about her riding and what she was doing to become the best rider at Canterwood. If Heather wasn't getting snarky comments from her mom, then she was getting grilled by her dad. No wonder she wanted someone—even someone she used to try to get kicked off the riding team—here with her during fall break.

We left the plate on the counter and started back toward my guest room.

Heather opened one of the doors in my room and flicked a switch, illuminating a giant walk-in closet.

"Start unpacking and hanging up your stuff," she said. "We've got a lot to do this week."

"I'm so excited to be back in the city," I said. "And to see your old stable."

Heather just nodded. She watched me unzip my suitcase, and I began taking out shirts and putting them on hangers.

She started pulling jeans, breeches, and pajamas out of my suitcase.

"Silver."

"What?" I turned away from the hangers and looked at her.

"*Please* tell me this isn't all you brought. You *did* bring clothes for dinner and going out, right?"

"Duh," I said. I rummaged through my suitcase and pulled out a flirty black skirt and a v-neck shirt. "This is totally cool for going out. I've got a great necklace that looks awesome with this shirt and—"

Heather raised a hand. "Stop. Now." She sighed and rubbed her forehead, squeezing her eyes together. "You brought *school* clothes, not New York City clothes. I'm *not* walking around Manhattan for a week with someone dressed like that."

I huffed and put a hand on my hip. "Then what am I supposed to do?"

"*You're* not doing anything. Tomorrow we're going

shopping. Like, ASAP. Until then you can borrow something of mine for dinner."

I wasn't going to turn down shopping, but I couldn't just stand there and let Heather get away with insulting my clothes.

"Fine, but—"

"Let's go. Besides, if you think this room is cool, wait till you see mine." Heather got up off the guest bed and walked toward the door.

I followed her, casting one last look back at my clothes. Whether or not I'd made the right decision to come, I was here now.

3

DINNER WITH
THE FOXES

I FOLLOWED HEATHER TO A ROOM DOWN ANOTHER hallway—they all looked the same!—and took a step backward when she pulled open double doors. Heather's room was like an oasis. Her bed was adorned with a black-and-red comforter and crisp white sheets. My feet sank into the bedroom's plush white carpet. Two black chairs surrounded a small coffee table in front of an enormous sliding glass door that led to a giant balcony.

"Bathroom's there if you're going to hurl from jealousy," Heather said, but her tone was teasing instead of mean.

"Your room is gorgeous," I said. "And you have your own private bathroom?"

Heather nodded. "Go see if you want."

I walked across the room and opened the door. A giant marble counter had two deep sinks. The shower was encased in glass, and there was another smaller counter with a chair tucked under it and a mirror surrounded by lights. Chanel, M.A.C., and Stila were among the half-dozen brands of cosmetics that lined the counter.

My fingers inched toward a cotton candy pink Clinique lip gloss.

"Try whatever," Heather said.

I jumped and turned toward her. She was resting against the doorjamb.

"I know you have, like, an untreatable addiction for gloss. Just put it back when you're done." I could barely breathe at the sight of the lip gloss she had. And I'd thought *my* collection was envy-worthy. Mine had nothing on Heather's.

I picked up the pink gloss and applied a thin coat to my lips. I checked my reflection in the mirror, smoothing my hair and wiping a few flakes of mascara from under my green eyes.

Reluctantly I left the bathroom and wandered back into Heather's bedroom. Light shone from an open door and I peered into a walk-in closet the size of my kitchen at home.

Rows and rows of shirts, pants, skirts, and dresses hung from wall to wall. A rack of folded sweaters towered over me. Shelves of boots, heels, flats, and shoes for every imaginable occasion were aligned perfectly along shelf after shelf.

And I thought Paige had a lot of clothes, I said. I shook the thought away. I was at Heather's—exactly where I needed to be to escape Paige, Jacob, and all the drama that lingered over the Canterwood Crest campus.

Heather shoved clothes to the side, obviously looking for something.

"I like clothes, but this is all my mom," she said, shaking her head. "It's ridic. I can't take all of these to school and I need to start, like, giving them away or something."

I touched a pair of red peep-toe kitten heels. "Maybe. But she's obviously thinking about you when you're not here and that's why she's getting you stuff."

Heather laughed. "Puh-lease. *She* doesn't get me any of this." She yanked a shirt off the hanger, and the black boat-neck shirt dangled from her fingertips. "*This* came from my mother's personal shopper. My mom has nothing to do with picking out my clothes. She just tells Sienna to get whatever is in style and buy it."

"But that's pretty cool! You get New York City clothes sent to you that no one else has."

Heather started to say something, but pressed her lips together. "Yeah," she said finally. She turned back to the clothes rack and shuffled through a bunch of dresses. She pulled out a royal blue cap-sleeve dress and handed it to me.

"There. Think you can manage to pair that with the right accessories?"

That I could manage.

"Yeees," I said, instantly regretting my snarky tone. Heather *was* trying to help. "Thanks for the dress. I should have thought to bring something fancier—I didn't think I'd need it."

"Manhattan mistake number one," Heather said. "You always need something glam on hand or you'll be . . . well, caught like you just were."

I looked up and saw a shelf at the back of Heather's closet that glittered with gold and silver trophies. Stepping around Heather, I walked over to the shelf and reached for a trophy.

I took one and, holding it, read the plaque. *First place: Floor exercise*.

I glanced up at Heather. "Floor exercise? Like, gymnastics?"

Heather shrugged and pulled her blond hair into a

loose, messy ponytail. "Yeah. I used to do gymnastics before I rode horses."

"You did?" I stared at her, shocked. "I never knew that."

Heather looked up at the trophies—polished and gleaming. She looked lost in thought for a second before she took the trophy from my fingers and put it back on the shelf. Heather turned and walked out of the closet. I followed her, laying the dress on the bed, and we sat in the chairs overlooking the balcony. The Manhattan skyline stretched out in front of us, and I looked down at my hands, unsure what to say—if anything.

Finally Heather sighed. "I did gymnastics before I even knew what a bridle was," she said without looking at me. "I loved it so much. I spent every second I could at the gym with my friends, practicing."

"I've watched some of the Olympic gymnastics," I said. "What were you the best at? Like, floor or beam?"

She looked at me with typical Heather cockiness. "All of them. Please."

Her answer made me grin. "Sor-*ry*."

Heather glanced at her closed bedroom door, then drew her legs up to her chest. "I loved every second of gymnastics. I had a great coach and she encouraged me to compete. I spent a lot of weekends on the road with

my team and we traveled everywhere for competitions."

"Sounds like you worked as hard at that as you do at riding," I said.

"I did."

I shifted in my chair, wondering if she'd keep talking if I just listened.

Heather's blue eyes focused on something in the distance. "I was at my friend Isobel's house and a bunch of us were sleeping over to celebrate a championship win. She had horses for pleasure riding and asked if anyone wanted to ride."

I nodded. Heather had *never* talked to me at this length before. Ever.

"And let me guess," I said. "You were the first one up for the challenge."

Heather smiled. "Of course I was. I was the only one who wanted to try it—the other girls were too afraid of getting injured before a gymnastics competition. But I wasn't scared. Isobel let me ride her horse, a Quarter horse–Arab mix, and we went on a trail ride. Everything felt . . . natural to me. I fell in love with riding and knew I *had* to convince my parents to let me ride."

We both jumped when someone knocked on Heather's door.

"Come in," Heather said.

Kay peered inside, smiling at us. "Need anything?"

Heather looked at me and I shook my head.

"We're good, thank you," Heather said.

Kay nodded and closed the door behind her.

"Did you think it would be hard to convince your parents to let you ride? I mean, was your dad focused on making sure you were only serious about gymnastics?" I asked Heather.

"I had to make a deal," Heather said. "Three extra hours in the gym every week if I wanted to ride for an hour every Saturday."

I shook my head. "How old were you?"

Heather shrugged. "Eight or nine, I guess."

I felt for her, but I didn't dare say it. If I did, Heather would say she didn't want my pity and she'd toss me out of her room.

"So you obviously took the deal and started riding," I said.

Heather and I gazed at the balcony as a pigeon flew up to the rail and perched there. The fat gray bird didn't even look at us.

"It was worth it." Heather paused and played with her ponytail.

I felt as though I had to say *something*. Something to assure her that she could trust me.

"I'm not going to tell anyone about this," I said. "You know I won't."

Heather stared at me. "I know you won't 'cause you'd be afraid for your life if you did." She smiled sweetly at me.

I laughed. "Exactly." And yeah, that was kind of true.

Heather got up and walked over to the cabinet near her desk. She opened the doors and revealed a violet mini-fridge. She grabbed two Cokes and handed me one.

"Thanks."

We took a few sips and Heather set down her can. "I really only wanted to ride for fun. It was one hour every week that I had to myself. I rode this suuuuper old Appaloosa gelding and got basic lessons so the stable owner would let me go on group trail rides."

I grinned. "I love that image. Was he able to trot at least?"

"Shut up," Heather said, but she laughed. "He could trot—so there. Anyway, after a few weeks the instructor called my parents and told them she thought I had natural talent for riding and she wondered if I was interested in trying one-on-one lessons and seeing how that would go."

"Was your dad immediately like, 'No way'?" I asked, sipping my Coke.

"He said no at first, but I guess my instructor told him I might have the potential to be a good rider."

I nodded. "That was all he needed to hear, right?"

Heather took a long drink. "Yep. I started taking lessons a couple of times a week, entered my first show, and won. I loved gymnastics, but it became really obvious that I was a better rider, even in a short amount of time, than I was a gymnast."

"So did you try to juggle both?"

Heather shook her head. "I couldn't. It was too many hours at the gym and the stable and with school . . . it was too much. I quit gymnastics and started riding full-time."

"Did you miss it? Did your dad care that you quit?" All of this was new to me, and I had so many questions.

"Omigod, you're, like, Oprah right now," Heather said. She tilted her head at me. "I missed it for a while, but I fell in love with riding. And my dad really didn't care what I did—as long as I was the best at it. And I guess I'm like him—'cause I wanted to be the best. And riding was it for me."

That was Heather Fox. The cutthroat, win-at-all-costs girl who knew how to excel at whatever she did. I envied that about her sometimes—not the way she handled some competitions or the way she treated a lot of people, but her confidence.

"Gross," Heather said, getting up. "*That* was, like, a lame Lifetime movie. Go unpack your . . . 'clothes,' get ready for dinner, and come back. I'll tell you all you need to know for dinner with the Foxes."

4

TRAPPED IN
THE FOX DEN

I GRABBED MY MAKEUP CASE, FLAT IRON, and Heather's dress and tiptoed down the hallway to the guest bathroom. When I clicked the lock, the tightness in my chest eased a little. I hadn't wanted another run-in with Mrs. Fox so soon. I sat at the edge of the claw-foot bathtub, sighing and looking at the bathroom's decor. There were cream-colored hand towels that looked too expensive to use, a dish of tiny soaps that *definitely* had to be for decoration, and a glass cabinet filled with bath towels. Beside the cabinet, a wicker basket overflowed with body wash, shampoo, and conditioner with French names that I couldn't even begin to pronounce.

For a second I wished Paige were here. She'd know what to do and how to handle, well, *everything*. Paige, a true Manhattan girl, had been to every type of soirée from the Lower East Side to SoHo and she'd know exactly what to do at a fancy dinner. I sighed and slid out of my clothes, picking up Heather's dress. I didn't want to be thinking about Paige or wishing she were here. I wanted her to apologize for our fight at the Homecoming dance. *But she'd tried that night and you didn't let her,* I told myself.

I slipped into Heather's dress and vowed to stop thinking about Paige.

I looked in the mirror and ran my hands over the blue fabric, smoothing the dress. My hair had started to get a little wavy, so I spent extra time flat-ironing it. It felt like I was getting ready for an important Canterwood dance or something. I hadn't put on much makeup this morning because I'd been in a hurry to get out of my dorm room . . . and away from Jacob, Eric, Callie, and all the discomfort at school.

I washed my face and started over with my makeup. I dotted concealer under my eyes, put on a light coat of dark brown mascara, dusted NARS blush across my cheeks, and applied a coat of Bonne Bell Lip Glam in Iced Pomegranate. It was pink, but not too bright, and had just a hint of sparkle. I didn't think Heather's parents would be impressed if I showed up for dinner wearing lots of makeup.

I stayed in the bathroom as long as I could, taking twice the amount of time I usually spent on hair and makeup, but still looking the same as I always did.

Just go out there, already. It wasn't time for dinner yet and maybe being around Heather would make me less nervous. I left the bathroom, put my clothes in a neat pile on top of my suitcase, and put on a pair of small, silver hoop earrings before wandering back to Heather's room.

"Hey," I said as I walked inside.

Heather looked me up and down, nodding in approval. "That actually looks good on you."

"Gee, thanks." I sat at the end of her bed.

Heather had changed into a royal purple cocktail dress and had paired it with a gold drop necklace that warmed her skin tone. She walked over to one of the chairs facing the balcony and turned it toward me when she sat down.

"Just because I don't want you to embarrass me at dinner, I'm going to give you the rundown on how it's going to go, 'kay?" Heather asked.

I nodded. "Okay." My voice was squeaky.

Heather took a breath and held up a manicured finger. "First, my dad has sworn he'll make it to dinner on time.

He knows my mom *hates* it when he's late. But guess what? He's, like, never home before ten. So Mom will already be in a bad mood before dinner starts because she's going to make us wait for him."

"Maybe your dad will call and tell her he's going to be late," I said.

Heather closed her eyes, rubbing her forehead. "That's not my dad's style. He comes home when he wants. Half the time Mom isn't here anyway. Whatever—it doesn't even matter."

"Sorry," I said quietly.

Heather glared at me. "Puh-lease. Waste your sympathy on someone who needs it. I'm just telling you this so you know what to expect."

"Right. Totally."

Heather played with her necklace. "So while we're waiting for Dad, my mom will tell endless stories about how she was a Canterwood legacy and how *I* should be doing as many social activities as I can besides riding. You know, to keep up the good family name."

I wanted to ask Heather why her mom didn't care that her daughter was happy as a rider, but I didn't want Heather to stop dispensing advice.

"The last thing to know," Heather said, "is that my

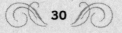

mom is going to . . ." She paused for a second. "She's going to, well, try to make you feel exactly like I did when you first came to Canterwood."

I gulped and my palms started sweating.

"Let's go," Heather said. "It's time for dinner with the Foxes."

I followed Heather out of her bedroom and to the massive dining room. A giant chandelier hung above the table. Placemats, silverware, empty glasses, cloth napkins, and china plates were already on the table. Heather sat in one of the high-backed chairs. I took a seat next to her and looked down. There was a soup bowl, a small plate, and a dinner plate underneath. But beside the plate were more forks, knives, and spoons than I'd ever seen.

"Are these all for me?" I whispered to Heather, even though no one else was in the room.

Heather leaned over. "Start from the outside. Forks—salad, dinner, dessert." She pointed to each one on the left side of my plate. "Soup, dinner spoon, and the knife is obvious."

"I'm never going to remember that!" I tried to fight back the panicky feeling in my chest.

"Just watch me."

Heather looked away when Mrs. Fox walked into the

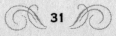

dining room. She sat across from Heather and stared at both of us. I was sure her eyes lingered on my— well, Heather's—dress for a second, but she didn't say anything.

Heather reached for her napkin and smoothed it onto her lap. Copying her, I did the same.

I felt like I could hear my own heartbeat in the silence. I looked up in relief when one of the staff walked into the room. She wore a black skirt and a starched white shirt. Her dark brown hair was back in a tight bun.

"Mrs. Fox," said the woman. "Would you like to begin with soup and salad?"

Mrs. Fox looked up at the woman and shook her head. "Are you not able to follow simple instructions, Helen?"

Helen seemed to shrink a little and she bowed her head.

"I'm sorry, Mrs. Fox. I didn't want your dinner to be late and—"

Mrs. Fox waved her hand, the massive diamond ring on her finger sparkling in the light. "I don't want to hear excuses, nor do I have time for them. I specifically told you to begin serving when my husband arrives."

Whhhoooa.

Mrs. Fox wasn't even talking to me and *I* was scared! I

almost couldn't believe what I'd just heard. I felt a rush of sympathy for Helen. I couldn't imagine speaking like that to anyone—ever!

Helen, red-faced, disappeared into the kitchen.

I shot a look at Heather and she stared at her empty soup bowl, her face pink. If that's how her mother acted when there was a guest in the house, I didn't even want to imagine how she treated the staff when no one was around.

"I hope it's now clear to everyone," Mrs. Fox said, "that we'll be waiting for Mr. Fox. He's likely caught in traffic, but should be arriving soon."

Heather and I didn't say anything. We kept our eyes down.

I shifted in my seat, knowing the sophisticated thing to do would be to engage Mrs. Fox in conversation about something like . . . art? Or opera? But I didn't know much (read: anything) about those. Or, at least, not much beyond van Gogh and *The Phantom of the Opera*—the movie version.

"Whatever scent's coming from the kitchen smells amazing," I said. "What are we having?"

Mrs. Fox turned her gaze to me. She had the same blue eyes as Heather, but unlike her daughter's, the iciness never melted.

"I think we can wait to discuss dinner until Mr. Fox arrives," Mrs. Fox said. I blushed and sank into my chair. She looked away from me and stared at the giant wall clock. It was almost seven. Mrs. Fox turned back to me and I wondered why I'd ever opened my mouth. I placed my elbow on the table, then whipped it off, hoping Mrs. Fox hadn't seen me.

"Do you plan on taking advantage of Canterwood's etiquette classes?" Mrs. Fox asked me. "When I attended the institution, I led etiquette courses by the time I was a sophomore."

"Um."

Argh! I wanted to smack myself in the face for saying "um." That was such a don't.

"I haven't taken any and I really haven't thought about it," I said. "My schedule's full right now with riding and my other classes."

Mrs. Fox raised both waxed eyebrows. "One shows quite a high level of confidence to think he or she is above etiquette courses."

"Oh, no," I said quickly. "I'm sure I do—I just haven't—"

"Mom," Heather interrupted. "Can we talk about something else, please?"

The chill I felt from Mrs. Fox's gaze shifted to Heather.

"Fine, Heather," Mrs. Fox said. "We haven't discussed Homecoming. I knew my daughter would win, but that *boy* who won—Jackson something—was he a worthy Prince?"

"It's Jacob, actually," Heather said.

His name was enough to make me blink. Jacob, who wanted me back. Jacob, who had left me at the Sweetheart Soirée, dated my other best friend, Callie, broke up with her, and then asked me to try again with him. My mind couldn't stay focused on Heather's convo with her mom. I saw Jacob's green eyes, his light brown hair that sometimes flopped into his eyes, and the way he smiled at me.

I'd been beyond devastated when Jacob had broken up with me at the Sweetheart Soirée last February, even though we hadn't technically been BF/GF. Then Eric— sweet, horse-crazy Eric—had come into my life and made me the happiest I'd ever been. But like my relationship with Jacob, it had been destroyed. There was no going back, even if I'd wanted to be Eric's girlfriend again.

"Heather!" Mrs. Fox's sharp tone yanked me out of my thoughts.

"You must realize that being Homecoming Princess comes with a long list of responsibilities," Mrs. Fox continued. "You now represent your eighth-grade class. When

you go back to school, everyone will look to you for how to dress, act, and behave."

I glanced at Heather and knew the look on her face. She wanted to argue. Wanted to say she never wanted to be Homecoming anything and wasn't at all interested in her "responsibilities" as Princess. But instead Heather just nodded.

"I know, Mom," Heather said.

Mrs. Fox glanced at the clock again. Seven fifteen. "I cannot imagine what's keeping your father," she said. "Excuse me—I'm going to call the office."

As Mrs. Fox left the room, Heather sighed. "This is only the beginning," she said, looking over at me. "She's not going to reach my dad and she'll come back even more upset."

"But you said this will probably be the only dinner we have with them," I said. "At least there's that."

"Yeeeah."

I reached for my water glass, then changed my mind. What if I dropped it? I envisioned water spilling over the Martha Stewart–perfect table.

A door slammed and Heather and I both jumped. Mrs. Fox strode into the dining room and tipped her chin up as she sat down.

"Your father's secretary said he had a last-minute conference call and will be at least another hour," Mrs. Fox
said.

"Mom, can't we just start?" Heather asked. "Dad won't
care."

"Heather, don't be rude," Mrs. Fox said. "An hour isn't
that long of a wait."

She looked at me and I squeezed my hands together
under the table.

"So, Sasha, you're a new . . . *friend* of my daughter's."

She said "friend" as if she were talking about something gross.

I nodded. "Yes, Heather and I are on the riding team
together and we recently—"

"You're a transfer student, correct?" Mrs. Fox asked,
interrupting me.

"That's right," I said. I tried not to be thrown off by
her question. "I started at Canterwood last year."

Deciding to be brave, I reached for my water glass and
took a long sip, hoping that was the end of the questions.

Mrs. Fox sat up straighter and tilted her head. "And
where did you live prior to transferring to Canterwood?"

"Union, Connecticut," I said.

"So did you travel to attend Dalton? Or Easterly?"

Mrs. Fox named two fancy private schools that were at least an hour away from my house.

"Uh, no," I said. "I attended public school in Union."

Mrs. Fox leaned back slightly, as if it were taking everything she had not to recoil in horror. Maybe she'd learned that in etiquette class.

Heather had been right—her mom was making me feeling exactly like Heather had during my first day at Canterwood. As if I was a small-town hick who didn't belong and had no right to be walking on Canterwood's prestigious campus.

"Public school," Mrs. Fox said slowly. "I can only imagine what an experience that must have been for you."

I tried not to look as angry as I felt. I was *so* over people dissing my hometown. Just because it wasn't Manhattan didn't make it the go-to topic for mocking.

"Union Middle School was great," I said, trying not to sound defensive. "I loved all of my teachers and everything I learned there has helped me at Canterwood."

Mrs. Fox pursed her lips. "I'm sure no matter how good your school seemed, you must have felt overwhelmed by a new environment. There would be nothing wrong if you were still having trouble adjusting to Canterwood."

"Mom," Heather interrupted. "Can we *please* eat? You

know Dad's not going to make dinner and I'm starving."

Mrs. Fox started to shake her head, then she took a deep breath. "Fine, Heather. There's no need to act immature over waiting for dinner."

Almost as if she'd been waiting on the other side of the kitchen door, anticipating instructions, Helen appeared and stood by Mrs. Fox.

"May I bring you anything, Mrs. Fox?" Helen asked.

"Yes, Helen," Mrs. Fox said, her voice sharp. "You may have the servers bring the salad and soup."

Helen scurried into the kitchen, and servers came into the dining room to collect our plates and bowls. Minutes later a steaming bowl of green soup and a romaine lettuce salad topped with bits of carrots, onions, mushrooms, cucumbers, and a half dozen other ingredients was set in front of me. Tiny glass salad-dressing bottles were lined up on the center of the table, and I tried not to stare at everything laid in front of me.

I watched Heather reach for the spoon on the far outside of her plate. Mimicking her, I did the same.

"This soup looks amazing," I said, smiling at Mrs. Fox.

"Curried split-pea soup is one of Mr. Fox's favorites," Mrs. Fox replied.

I dipped in my spoon, determined not to slurp when I brought it to my mouth.

I'd never had split-pea soup, let alone *curried* split-pea soup. It was hot, but not too spicy. I took another taste and liked it more with each swallow. We ate our soup in silence, then moved on to the salad.

I poured ranch dressing on mine. Heather reached for the same and pulled back her hand when Mrs. Fox frowned at her. Instead, Heather took the Italian dressing and put a couple of drops on her salad. I almost choked on my bite of lettuce, feeling a rush of sympathy for Heather.

I couldn't wait for dinner to be over.

We ate our salads, and the instant we'd all finished, our plates were cleared and the servers started bringing the next course. The smell of chicken wafted through the air and I sniffed appreciatively.

Mrs. Fox didn't pick up her fork and knife until she, Heather, and I were the only ones in the room.

"What is this, Mom?" Heather asked. "It looks new."

Mrs. Fox nodded. "It is. I got the recipe from Anne—you remember her from the country club—and gave it to our cook. It's hazelnut-encrusted chicken with raspberry sauce."

"Mmm," I said. "That sounds great."

Mrs. Fox ignored me and took a dainty bite of chicken. No one spoke throughout the main course. I made sure I took tiny bites and kept my mouth closed while I chewed. I was reaching for my water glass when Mr. Fox strode into the living room. He was dressed exactly like the men I'd seen on TV who worked high-powered jobs in NYC. His tie was stark white against his black shirt and black suit jacket. His dark hair was cropped short.

He handed his leather briefcase with shiny gold locks to Kay and she left the room. Mr. Fox kissed his wife on the cheek and sat at the head of the table.

"How was your conference call?" Mrs. Fox asked.

Something in her tone made me think she wasn't so much asking about the call, but rather, why he'd missed dinner.

"Productive," Mr. Fox said. He gave Heather a half smile, and then seemed to notice me for the first time. "Sasha, correct?"

"Yes, sir," I said. "Thank you for letting me stay during break. My parents and I really appreciate it."

Mr. Fox nodded. "We're happy to welcome you into our home, but this is *not* a break."

I didn't know what else to do but stare at him. What *did* he think this was?

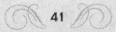

"This is a break from classes," Mr. Fox continued. "But Heather will not stop practicing her riding." He turned to look at his daughter. "With a week off school, I expect you to be in the arena more. I've already arranged for horses to be available so you'll be able to practice."

"I know, Dad," Heather said. "I promised I was going to ride more. I will. And Sasha's riding too. We're both working toward the upcoming schooling show."

"I don't want you distracted, Heather," Mr. Fox said.

Heather let out a barely audible sigh. "Dad, Sasha and I are both on the Youth Equestrian National Team. No one else at my old stable is at that level. I need someone to practice with."

Mr. Fox looked at her for a long second before finally nodding.

"All right. But I want full reports on what you're doing, and if we need to phone Mr. Conner over break to make sure you're doing enough, we will."

Heather didn't say anything—she just sat there. I squirmed in my seat, wanting to do something to get the attention off her. I knew the last thing she wanted was for her dad to call Mr. Conner, our riding instructor at Canterwood.

"I thought you were going to be on time for dinner," Mrs. Fox said, turning to her husband.

Okay, so I don't have to do a thing. Mrs. Fox is already taking care of the distraction.

"You know I can't leave work when York phones from London," Mr. Fox said. "It was an important call that I couldn't miss."

Mrs. Fox's eyes turned a shade colder. I hadn't thought that was possible.

"You went ahead and ate anyway, so it's not as though I delayed your meal," Mr. Fox said. "Besides, I ate a late lunch at the office and I'm more in the mood for coffee and dessert."

"Helen!" Mrs. Fox's yell made Heather and me jump.

The double doors to the kitchen swung open and Helen hurried through them.

"We're ready for dessert and coffee," Mrs. Fox instructed.

"Yes, ma'am," Helen said, tipping her head.

Dessert—crème brûlée and cappuccino—was served, and I was sure Heather and I had the same unspoken goal: to finish as fast as possible so we could get out of there! We gobbled our desserts, and I drank my cappuccino so fast that it burned my tongue.

Heather's parents didn't even look at each other as they finished their desserts.

"May we be excused?" Heather asked. "I want to study one of my DVDs from the last show."

Mr. Fox nodded. "You're excused."

"Thank you for the wonderful meal," I said, giving Mr. and Mrs. Fox a shaky smile. I hurried after Heather before Mrs. Fox could insult me again or Mr. Fox started grilling me about my own riding.

As soon we were out of the dining room, Heather slowed and turned to me.

"You *know* we're not spending valuable break time watching a dumb show DVD, right?"

"Figured."

"Go put on pj's and meet me in the TV room—it's past the living room. We can watch a movie."

"Sounds fun," I said.

"Anything sounds fun compared to that dinner," Heather said, faking a giant smile as she walked away to her room.

5

YOU'D THINK YOU'D HAVE LEARNED

BACK IN "MY" ROOM, I PULLED ON A PAIR of cozy pink pants and a white T-shirt with a tiny pocket. I put Heather's dress on a hanger and glanced around the room, making sure everything was neat in case Mrs. Fox had one of the maids inspect it or something.

I opened the door and listened, but didn't hear anyone. It felt as if I had to sneak around everywhere here! Crossing my fingers that her parents weren't anywhere near the TV room, I hurried down the hall and walked along the back of the living room to double doors that had to be for the TV room.

I put a hand on the doorknob, pausing and hoping I'd heard Heather's directions—

"Omigod," someone hissed in my ear. "Just stand there forever."

I jumped and my heart pounded as Heather pushed past me and opened the door.

I followed her inside and almost did one of those clichéd and embarrassing double takes when I looked around. Was *everything* in this apartment insanely cool?

A giant black couch with tables on either side was set up in front of a huge plasma TV mounted to the wall. There was a surround sound system that I knew was going to be amazing, and glass cabinets filled with DVDs lined a wall of the giant room. On the far side of the couch were a couple recliners with cup holders and outlets for headphones.

"This is awesome," I said. "It's better than any of Canterwood's media rooms."

Heather smiled. "Yeah, it's pretty cool. I used to spend a lot of time in here when I lived at home. My parents hardly ever use this room anymore, except when they're trying to impress their friends or something."

She motioned to the back of the room and I noticed a stainless steel fridge and a counter, microwave, and giant black cabinet.

"There's soda, popcorn, candy—tons of snacks back there. Get whatever and I'll pick out a flick."

"Okay, thanks," I said.

I knew Heather liked Diet Dr Pepper, so I grabbed two cans from the fridge and put them on a tray. Baskets filled with minipacks of chips, pretzels, Cheetos, and other movie food lined the counter. I filled the tray with a bunch of options and set it on the table in front of the couch. While I settled into the left side of the sofa, Heather stood in front of me and held up three DVDs.

"Got a vote?" she asked. "Even though I probably won't listen to you, anyway."

I pointed to a comedy on the far left. "I haven't seen that one."

Heather walked over to the DVD player. "Huh. Me either." She popped it in and flicked on the massive TV. The previews started and I opened a bag of chips.

"We better relax while we can," I said. "It sounds like we might be riding more this week than we do at school."

Heather snorted. "Please. It's called 'break' for a reason. I just told my dad that so he'd chill."

"So we're not riding?"

"I didn't say that. We—well, definitely *you*—need to practice and we're going to be riding. But not every second. There's too much to do this week."

I looked away from the TV to stare at her. "Like . . . what?"

"Silver, do you not know how to be quiet when a movie's on?"

I stared at her for another second before picking up a chip and focusing on the previews. Heather had *something* planned for this week. And knowing her, it was going to be good.

An hour and a half later the credits rolled, and Heather turned off the TV. We'd laughed through most of the movie and had eaten our way through the entire tray of food. My eyes had started to close during the final few minutes of the movie and I was surprised how tired I was this early—it was just after ten.

Heather yawned and stretched her arms. "I'm going to bed. And you should too. Be ready for breakfast by eight and we'll be out of here by nine."

"Out to where?" I asked.

Heather got up off the couch, shaking her head. "You'd think you'd have learned by now." She started toward the door, turning back to grin at me. "'Night, Silver."

I sat there staring after her. I couldn't even imagine what she had planned for tomorrow, but I wasn't going to be yawning my way through it.

I got up, walked to the guest room, and gathered my

toothbrush and face wash. In the bathroom I brushed my teeth and washed my face. I stared into my reflection, trying to breathe and not worry about whatever Heather had planned for tomorrow. When I climbed into bed, my nerves melted slowly into excitement. After all, this *was* New York City.

6

STOP TALKING

I ROLLED OVER IN BED AS SUNLIGHT FILTERED through the venetian blinds. Wait. *Venetian blinds?* I blinked and sat up in bed, looking around at the room.

Ohhh. For a second I'd forgotten where I was.

I leaned back against the down pillow and took a breath. I was at Heather's. I hadn't slept over at many people's houses before and it felt strange to wake up in an unfamiliar place.

I rolled over, staring at the clock. Seven fifteen. Heather had said breakfast was at eight and I *so* didn't want to be late. I went through my suitcase, unsure what to choose since Heather hadn't exactly been clear about what we were doing today.

I finally settled on dark-wash skinny jeans, a clover

green shirt, and platform sandals. I carried my clothes to the bathroom and emerged twenty minutes later, washed, dressed, and ready for breakfast.

I walked down the hallway and, smiling, sidestepped a maid I hadn't seen yesterday. Just how much help *did* the Foxes have?

"Good, you're actually up," Heather said, following me down the hall. She was dressed in black skinny jeans, sandals, and a red shirt. "I thought I'd have to send Helen in to drag you out of bed."

I rolled my eyes. "How long have *you* been up, then? I'm just running into you in the hallway."

Heather glared at me. "Whatever. Let's eat and go already."

I followed Heather to a small, sunny room at the back of the penthouse. It was a cute breakfast area with a round table that sat four people. Two placemats were laid out on the table with bowls and silverware. There was a giant bowl of cut-up mixed fruit in the center of the table.

"Told you it'd be the only meal we'd have with them," Heather said. Her tone was light, but I could tell it bothered her. She acted as if she didn't care that her parents were involved in her life only when it came to being

Homecoming Princess or a champion rider. But she *did* care and it did affect her.

Helen walked into the room and smiled at us. "What can I get you girls for breakfast?" she asked.

"A Belgian waffle, please," Heather said.

Helen nodded. "And, Sasha?" she asked. "I can make any type of waffle or pancake that you'd like. I can also make eggs or whatever else you normally eat for breakfast."

"Blueberry pancakes would be great," I said. "Thank you."

Heather reached the spoon into the fruit bowl and scooped cantaloupe, grapes, pineapple, banana, and strawberries, among other fruits, and passed me the spoon. I filled my bowl with the fresh fruit and speared a piece of mango. Yum.

"So are you going to tell me what store we're going to, or are you going to blindfold me till we get there?" I asked.

Heather ate two bites of fruit before looking at me. "A store that will fix *that*."

"What?"

"That." Heather waved her hand at me.

I shook my head. "I have *no* idea what you're talking about."

"Your outfit, Silver."

"What's wrong with this?" I looked down at myself. "I definitely want to go shopping and get some things for school, but there's nothing wrong with my wardrobe."

"Sasha, I've already explained this. Those clothes are acceptable for school, but you're in NYC. With *me*." Heather shuddered as if she felt a chill.

I sighed. "Whatever. At least my parents gave me shopping money for the trip, so I'll be able to get a ton of stuff."

"How much?" Heather asked. She scooped up the last bit of honeydew melon from her bowl.

"A hundred dollars," I said proudly. "They *never* give me that much. I'll probably, like, go crazy."

Heather folded her arms across her chest, an amused smile on her face.

"Oh, Sasha Silver from Union," she said. "A hundred won't even buy a heel where we're going."

I blinked. "But—I—"

"Here you go, girls!" Helen said, walking into the room with our breakfast. She set down a plate of three steaming blueberry pancakes and put tiny containers of butter and syrup between Heather and me. She also served Heather her waffle.

"Thank you," Heather and I said. Heather reached for the butter, and I couldn't stop staring at her.

"Wait, wait," I said. "That conversation soo wasn't over. I have *one hundred dollars*"—I said those three words slowly—"to spend. That's it. I mean, we couldn't rack up a bill like that at Express or H & M that easily."

Heather almost dropped her fork. She covered her eyes with her hands, breathed for a few seconds, then shook her head at me.

"It's actually kind of cute that you think we'd go to Express or H & M," she said.

"Forever 21?" I asked.

Heather stabbed a bite of her waffle. "Stop talking and eat so we can go."

I shrugged and finished my beyond-amazing pancakes.

"Let's grab our purses and get out of here," Heather said.

We went to our rooms, got our purses, and headed for the front door.

"Heather?"

I jumped and we both turned to see Mrs. Fox staring at us. She had a leather day planner in one hand and a fountain pen in the other.

"Where are you going?" Mrs. Fox continued.

Heather flashed a smile. "We're going shopping. I thought I needed some new clothes when I go back to school, since I'm Homecoming Princess now."

Her reason for shopping was a total lie. I watched Mrs. Fox's face to see if she'd buy it.

"That sounds like a good idea," Mrs. Fox said. "Make sure you don't get anything in yellow. You know how that looks with your skin tone."

"I know, Mom. I won't," Heather said, still maintaining the fake cheeriness. "See you later."

Mrs. Fox just nodded and disappeared before we'd even put on our shoes. Mom and Dad would have wanted to know everywhere I was going—they'd *never* let me leave like that in Union, let alone New York City. But I didn't say that to Heather.

We walked out the door and I felt like I could breathe better when we got out of the penthouse. The hallway was quiet and the building's lobby had a few people entering and exiting. The doorman pulled open the door for Heather and me, and we stepped through, smiling our thanks.

At just after nine, the city air was chilly, and sunlight found its way around the tall buildings and filtered down to us.

"Which way's the subway?" I asked, looking in both directions. I'd ridden the subway once with Paige over the summer. We'd told her parents we were using a car service, but I'd begged Paige to take me on the subway and she'd agreed. It had been so much fun. I stood still—frozen in the memory. We'd bought single-ride MetroCards and had ridden the F train to a stop close to Paige's before using a car service.

I jolted out of my thoughts when I realized Heather was standing in front of me, staring at me.

"The *subway*?" she asked.

"Ooh," I teased. "Sorry. Is the subway not a Park Ave thing to do?"

Heather glared, but I saw a hint of a smile. "The subway is *never* the thing to do," she said. "You're so lucky I'm actually willing to teach you about how to really live in NYC. Otherwise . . ." She just shook her head.

"So we hail a taxi?" I said it with a straight face, knowing she'd use a car service.

Heather groaned and spun away from me. She punched numbers on her phone, and then slid it shut.

"We're using the family's car," Heather said. "We will *not* be"—Heather took a breath—"riding the subway or sitting in the back of some disgusting taxi.

I can't believe you'd ever even think I'd do those things."

I laughed to myself and pretend bowed to her. "I apologize, Miss Fox, for expecting you to do something, oh, I don't know, normal."

Heather started to say something back, but as she opened her mouth, the sleek car we'd ridden in yesterday appeared. The same driver got out and hurried to open the door to the backseat.

Heather got in first and I started to climb in after her, expecting her to move over.

"I. Do. Not. Slide," Heather said. "Walk around."

"Oookkaaay." I held up my hands and walked to the car's other back door. The driver was already waiting with the door open. "I'm Sasha," I said. I figured I'd be seeing a lot of him this week, so he should at least know my name.

"And I'm Paul," he said, tipping his hat to me.

I smiled and climbed into the car. Paul got into the driver's seat and looked back to Heather.

"Where can I take you?" he asked.

"Let's start with Barneys," Heather said.

"To Madison Avenue it is," Paul said. He turned back around and the car rolled forward smoothly.

Barneys. Wow. I didn't want to say that out loud and

look like a total loser to Heather. But *wow!* I'd never been to Barneys. That was a store that required serious glossing before entering.

I reached into my purse and dug around for a lip gloss. I put back two before finding the one I wanted—Kiss This Gloss in Smooch. It was shimmery with a tint of rosy pink. I applied the gloss—making sure it wasn't smeary— and had just snapped my compact shut when Paul pulled the car to the curb.

"I'll text you when we're done," Heather said, leaning forward. "Thanks, Paul."

Paul nodded. "Have fun, ladies."

Heather turned to me. "I'm going to open my door since it's away from the street, and this time, you *can* get out after me."

She got out of the car and I followed her, closing the door behind me. Paul pulled back into traffic, and Heather and I were alone on Madison Avenue. I glanced up at the green street sign, and the words "Madison Avenue" stared back at me. It made me smile—I loved New York.

"Silver!" Heather said. She grabbed my elbow and pulled me forward. "People are going to think you're weird if you just stand there staring at a *street sign*."

"Sorry," I said. "But you're used to this. I'm not. It's still a big deal."

The look on Heather's lightly tanned face softened. "Yeah, fine. Okay. But it's way better inside, so let's go."

"Okay."

We walked down the sidewalk, weaving around people, and walked toward a red awning that said BARNEYS NEW YORK. Under the awning, a giant window display showed three mannequins dressed like models from a Paris runway. I almost stopped walking, but there were so many people on the street, I didn't want to get run over. We walked under a second awning, and the beyond-brilliant shade of red didn't impress me any less the second time I saw it. This window display showed off crisp men's suits that looked like clothes you'd see at the Oscars.

I followed Heather up to the one-story-high glass entrance, and we walked through the revolving door. I walked a few feet before I stopped. Someone clipped my shoulder.

"Sasha! God!" Heather said. "Act like you've been in a store before. You can't stop in the middle of the doorway."

But I barely heard Heather. Barneys was *insane*. And I was only five feet inside the door. I wasn't a shopaholic, but this place could make me one, considering we were

only on the first of what looked like many floors.

"C'mon," Heather said. "This is where all of the tourists walk around in a daze—like you're doing now. I know exactly where we need to go."

Heather navigated the crowd with ease and I followed behind her. I noticed how everything about the way she moved screamed *New Yorker*. She didn't sidestep anyone, but didn't plow through the crowd either. She walked with purpose and knew exactly where she was going. I felt like a puppy tagging along behind her. I tried to copy her posture—head up, shoulders back—and the look I was sure was on her face: a cool disinterest in the people around her.

We walked past counters of makeup and skin products. I couldn't even read all of the brands—I had to focus on Heather so I didn't get lost in the crowd.

"Sample, miss?" a woman asked Heather. She spritzed a tab of paper with perfume and held it out to Heather.

Heather walked past without even stopping.

We passed the M.A.C. counter, where a woman was sitting in a chair, having blush brushed onto her cheeks by a makeup artist. Women were hovering over the makeup counters, pointing at shades of lipstick, types of moisturizer, and different tints of concealer.

Heather and I made it to the elevator and she pushed the up button.

"We're starting with the second floor," Heather said. "Sienna works that floor and she'll give us special attention."

"Like, she'll help us find sizes?" I asked.

The elevator doors opened, and Heather and I squeezed inside the crowded elevator. Someone had already pushed the button for the second floor.

"Like, she'll make sure dressing rooms are always empty for us and she'll help us find the perfect clothes," Heather said. "It's actually always been really fun when I've done it."

"That's so cool," I said. "We have our own personal shopper."

The elevator doors opened, and Heather and I got off with a few people.

"All the clothes we need are on this floor," Heather explained. "They've got all the best stuff. We need to walk back to the customer-service counter."

"Lead the way," I said.

Heather was excited about this—there was no denying that. She'd always dressed well at school—not like a fashionista but like someone who knew what she was doing. I wondered if that entire time it had been Mrs. Fox's personal shopper choosing and sending the clothes.

"Sienna's the coolest," Heather said as we walked down the aisle. "She knows exactly what I like."

"So . . ." I didn't want to start a fight with her, but I had to ask. "Do you like clothes and shopping when *you* do it, instead of someone doing it for you?"

Heather rubbed her glossed lips together. "Yeah," she said. "I guess I like choosing styles and things that I like, instead of having clothes handed to me."

We reached the counter and waited while the sales-clerk helped someone in front of us. It sounded like a fantasy having someone pick out clothes for you and knowing they'd look good. But the more I listened to Heather, the more I realized that wasn't true. I wondered if a sense of individuality was lost when someone else was making all of your choices. I didn't study fashion magazines, but I liked clothes and had fun piecing things together.

The woman in front of us finished her conversation, and Heather and I moved up to the counter.

"Hi," Heather said to the clerk. "Could you let Sienna know Heather Fox is here?"

The woman nodded. "Certainly. One moment, please."

She picked up a phone and spoke quietly into it. She hung up and smiled at us. "Sienna will be right with you, Miss Fox. Please, may I take your purses until you're finished shopping?"

"Sure," Heather said. We handed our purses to the assistant and she disappeared into a back room.

"Is that safe?" I asked. "We just gave someone our purses. My new gloss is in there!" I blurted out the last sentence.

Heather looked at me, and for a second, I wondered if she was going to slap me. "Your *lip gloss* is safe, Silver. Trust me."

"Heather!" We both turned as a petite blonde hurried over and hugged Heather.

"Sienna, hi!" Heather said, hugging her back.

Sienna smiled at me and stuck out her hand. "I'm Sienna, obviously."

"I got that," I said, grinning. "I'm Sasha."

Sienna was dressed every bit the Barneys girl. Her spiky heels had to be at least four inches high. She wore a short skirt, ribbed black tights, and a simple white tank that was dressed up with a dozen layered necklaces. She looked amazing, but not like she was trying too hard in that annoying way.

Sienna looked at Heather with a sideways expression.

"So . . . are you here for something in particular, or are you here to—"

"Cause damage to the AmEx!" Heather and Sienna said at the same time, then they laughed.

"You know my mom," Heather said. "She gave me her black AmEx. She doesn't care what I put on it as long as it's 'proper' for school."

"Oh, I know," Sienna said. Her tone made me realize that she and Heather had some sort of understanding about Mrs. Fox and her need to dress Heather like a style snob.

"You'll love this," Heather said. "It's going to make your job *so* much easier."

Sienna raised an eyebrow. "I can't wait to hear this."

Heather gave a fake giant grin. "Guess who won Homecoming Princess?"

Sienna slapped her hand against the counter. "Omigod! No way." She put her hand over her heart in a mocking way. "Your dream come true."

Faking seriousness, Heather nodded. "Exactly. So of course my mom's going to expect even more 'princess-worthy' clothes."

Sienna put a hand to her chin. "We'll do that."

Heather's smile slipped.

"And we'll give that bag to your mom. And you can

take the clothes *you* want in another bag," Sienna finished.

That made Heather grin. "And that's why I'm glad to see you. It's perfect. She never checks the credit card statement anyway—she just pays it."

"Then let's shop!" Sienna said. "I'm going to clear two dressing rooms and reserve them. Be right back."

"Um, Heather," I said. "I'm totally into shopping, and I'd love to help you pick out stuff, but I told you what my budget is and—"

Heather shook her head. "Shut up. I'm using the AmEx on everything."

"No way," I argued. "I'm not letting you do that."

"You don't have a choice. I'm doing it. My parents *really* don't care."

"I can't have you buy my clothes," I said.

"I told you—I'm not walking around with you dressed like that. And here—think of it as a gift from them for being such jerks to you last night."

I paused, thinking about that last sentence.

"Okay," I said finally. "A *couple* of things. That's it."

Heather nodded. "Right. Fine. A couple of things."

Sienna walked over to us. "All right. I've put RESERVED signs on two of the rooms, so they're ready whenever you girls want to start trying on clothes."

"Thanks," Heather and I said.

"Where do you want to start?" Sienna asked.

Heather thought for a second. "Fall tops," she said. "Then skirts and pants."

Sienna nodded. "Let's do it."

Heather and I walked behind her, away from the customer-service desk. We passed brands I'd *never* heard of (dodo + angelika?!), and Sienna stopped in a section I *knew* was going to have price tags with four digits on them.

"I looove Maxx Aro's stuff," Sienna said. "I think it's a good place to start. His collection has everything— preppy for class, edgy for Friday nights, fun stuff for the weekends, and casual clothes."

"Let's start with stuff we can wear to class but also not look boring and blah," Heather said.

Sienna nodded. "Perfect. Let's talk colors that you like and that look good on you."

Heather grinned. "Well, *every* color looks good on me," she said, her expression teasing. "But I need more black, red, and cream in my wardrobe."

"Agreed," Sienna said. "And those are all fantastic colors with your skin tone." Sienna turned to me. "What about you, Sasha? What colors do you like?"

I paused, nervous about saying it out loud. What if

66

I told someone who knew fashion that I *thought* certain colors looked good on me but when really they looked horrible? "I like royal purple, hunter green, and black."

Sienna nodded immediately. "Light brown hair looks amazing with darker colors, and purple makes green eyes pop. You both go ahead and start looking, pull a bunch of pieces, and I'll pick out a few things that I think you should try. Then you'll try them on and we'll toss out anything we don't like."

"Perfect," Heather said.

We started wandering through the rows and rows and *rows* of clothes. I tried not to touch every sweater and shirt that I passed. Everything was so soft! I saw a deep green three-quarter-sleeve shirt with a v-neck. They had my size and it was the perfect cut and color. My fingers reached to check the price tag, but I stopped myself. *It's not going to be any fun if you do that the entire time,* I told myself. *You can do that at the end when you choose your clothes.* I nodded at my resolve. For now I was going to do exactly what Sienna had said to do—I was going to pick whatever looked like it might be a good match and go from there.

I wandered through the racks of shirts and the tables with folded sweaters. I picked up a black sweater that was simple but classic. It would go with almost anything, and

I had a silver necklace and drop earrings that would make it look amazing.

Then I saw a heather gray cardigan that was cut long and would look awesome with jeans during a casual weekend. I started to drape it over my arm when someone reached for it.

"Let me take this." It was Sienna. "I'll hang it up in your dressing room and that way your hands are free."

"Thanks," I said. I handed the clothes to her, and then I spotted a long-sleeve deep purple shirt with a scoop neck. I found my size and rubbed the fabric between my fingers. So. Soft.

I glanced up, looking around for Heather. She was holding a black wrap shirt in front of her.

I smiled to myself. This was way more fun than I'd thought it would be.

A seashell pink long-sleeve shirt, a sand-colored shrug, and a navy blue yoke sweater with white stitching were all taken from my arms and to the dressing room by Sienna.

And I kept adding clothes. *You're just trying them on, anyway,* I reminded myself. Like playing dress-up. I wasn't keeping even a tenth of this stuff.

A few minutes later, Heather wandered over to me. "I'm ready to start trying stuff on," she said. "You?"

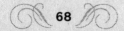

"Definitely," I said. "I've got more than enough."

Sienna was waiting by the dressing rooms. "Your initials are taped to your room," she said. "I put a few extra pieces in there. Start trying things on and come out and let's look at something when you think it's a possibility."

Heather and I passed several doors until we saw RESERVED: HF and RESERVED: SS taped on dressing rooms that were side by side.

"You better not come out in something that looks exactly like what you're wearing now," Heather said, smiling brightly as she shut her door behind her.

I entered my own dressing room. It was *huge*. It had a chair in the corner, a ledge to sit on, and several hooks to hang clothes on. In the corner was a three-way mirror that would show every angle of my body. I swallowed a little. That would make it *really* visible if I put on a dumb shirt or sweater.

Stop it and just start trying on clothes, I said to myself.

And I did. It took only a couple of seconds of glancing at an outfit to tell if it was worth exiting the dressing room or not. And I hadn't heard Heather come out yet either, so she was still searching for the right piece. I took the deep purple shirt off the hanger and pulled it over my head. Smoothing it, I looked in the mirror. Score!

I opened the door and Sienna got up from the bench she was sitting on between Heather and my dressing rooms.

"Love. It," Sienna said. "The color's perfect and I adore the cut. Great eye, Sasha."

I smiled. "Thanks!"

I started back to my room when Heather's door opened. She'd chosen a black v-neck long-sleeve shirt.

Sienna smiled. "And you guys need me *why*? That looks gorgeous, Heather. It's a definite."

"I really like it too," I said.

Heather eyed my purple shirt. "Thanks. I like yours, too. You could have ended up looking like a grape, but you didn't."

She disappeared back into her dressing room.

We repeated the process until we'd gone through all of the tops. I'd found three that I loved—the purple shirt, a black silk cardigan that Sienna had chosen, and the seashell-colored shirt.

Heather and I emerged with our items at the same time. I hadn't dared to look at the price tags yet. Heather had picked three things too. The black v-neck long-sleeve shirt, a deep red sweater, and a body-hugging dark gray belted sweater.

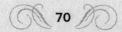

"Great choices, girls!" Sienna said. "Those will be perfect. They've got a mix of prep and edge. I'll meet you up at the register so you can drop those off and keep looking." Sienna left the dressing area, and I turned to Heather.

"I like these three," I said. "But I'm not letting you get all of them. So help me pick one."

Heather rolled her eyes. "Will you just shut up? You're getting them. So there."

"Heather—"

"I'm not continuing this convo. We're doing skirts next. Forget pants. Boring."

I took a breath, deciding not to argue. Heather and I gave our clothes to Sienna.

"We're doing skirts," Heather said. "I think we can handle that."

"Cool," Sienna said. "Come find me if you need anything."

Heather and I stuck together this time and looked through skirts. It didn't take us long to each find two that we loved.

"I think those'll look great," I said, nodding at Heather's choices of a flirty black skirt with an inch of lace at the bottom and a crimson mini that would be fun with tights for a weekend night out.

"Duh, I chose them," Heather said. She looked at

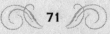

mine. I'd picked a ruffled black skirt and a sleek gray one that skimmed above my knees and was *so* soft. "Those don't look like they were handmade by your mom, so I think they're going to work for you."

We tried them on and emerged minutes later with skirts in hand. "I love them both," I said.

"Me too," Heather said. "Let's check out on this floor and go to shoes. I'm bored with clothes now."

"Okay," I said. We gave our skirts to Sienna and I looked away from the register as she rang up the total.

"It's going to be—" Sienna started.

Heather reached into her pocket and shoved the AmEx at Sienna before she could say the number. "Doesn't matter. Charge it."

Sienna swiped the card, Heather signed the receipt, and we grabbed our bags. Sienna hurried to the back room and brought us our purses.

"Thanks so much," I said.

"Of course," Sienna said. "Hope to see you back soon!"

"You will. And I'm sure you'll see my mother any day now," Heather said.

Sienna hid a smile. "I'm sure I will. Bye, girls."

Heather and I got in the much less crowded elevator and she pushed a button.

"Thank you," I said. "That was really nice of you. You didn't have to——"

Heather gave me a look that made me close my mouth. "You're welcome," she said. "But thank me again or argue about getting stuff and you'll wish you'd graciously accepted everything."

The girl was scary sometimes.

The elevator doors opened and we stepped onto the next floor.

Shoes.

Everywhere.

Stilettos.

Flats.

Boots.

Sandals.

"I need new fall boots," Heather said. She glanced down at my platform sandals. "And you obviously need new sandals and I'm going to just guess that you need boots."

"I have boots . . . they . . ." I paused, thinking. Groan—Heather was actually right. My boots were scuffed and pretty worn. "I need boots," I muttered.

Heather grinned. "Knew it."

We went straight to the boots. I picked up a pair of

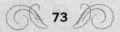

caramel-colored, butter-soft knee-high boots with a heel. A salesperson found my size, and I held one up to Heather.

"Thoughts, Shopping Yoda?"

Heather wrinkled her nose. "Please don't reference me to *Star Wars* or *Star Trek*. Whatever. But, yeah—I like those. Try them on."

I slid my feet into the boots and stood. I walked over to a mirror and checked them out. They looked hot.

"Nice job, Silver," Heather said. There was real approval in her tone. "You have to get them."

She sat down and slid her feet into a pair of dark brown slouch boots with a chunky heel. "I have enough in black," she said. She walked over to the mirror and stood next to me. We both looked at her boots.

"Those are awesome," I said. "They would look great with skinny jeans."

Heather nodded. "Yeah, they would, actually."

We gathered our boots and moved to the sandals. We tried on a bunch of pairs before we both settled on the right ones. I loved a pair of T-strap sand-colored wedges that had a cute buckle on the ankle. Heather had found a pair of dressy black mules with a skinny two-inch heel.

We checked out, and again I ignored the price and let Mrs. Fox's AmEx get a workout.

 74

Heather and I walked toward the elevator and she paused. "I was going to do accessories, but let's save that for another day. I don't want to, like, give you a shopping stroke."

I smiled. "Thanks. But how about when we do accessories, you let *me* pick where we go? I did just shop with you for hours with very little argument."

"Fiiine," Heather said. "But if you try to take me somewhere with used jewelry, you'll be dead."

"Deal," I said. "No used jewelry. I think I can manage that."

We got to the bottom floor and Heather pulled out her phone. "Let me text Paul. It'll take him two seconds to get here."

She texted and we walked out of Barneys. We'd no sooner reached the spot where he'd dropped us off than the Foxes' car pulled up beside the curb. I opened the door and slid inside, remembering Heather's "I don't slide" from earlier, and she got in after me.

"Looks like you girls had a successful afternoon," Paul said, glancing at our bags before easing into traffic.

"Totally," Heather said. She turned to me. "Huh."

"What?" I asked.

"I don't have to hide any of these clothes from my

mom. There's nothing in here that would freak her out."

I thought about what she'd picked out. "True. That's funny. Maybe your tastes are more similar than you realized."

Heather gave me a death stare.

"I take it back! I take it back," I said, laughing. "Your mom *def* wouldn't have picked out the miniskirt."

"So. True," Heather said. She combed through her bag and gave it to me. "Put it in your bag and I'll get it from you later."

I stuck the skirt between my shirts and sank back into the leather seat. I'd never be able to be one of those stuck-up socialites who shopped all day. I was tired! Shopping was oddly exhausting. All the trying on clothes and all the walking—we'd probably covered five miles inside Barneys.

We pulled up to Heather's building and I gathered my bags. Paul got out of the car and opened Heather's door. She exited gracefully and I waited for my turn to get out. I smiled my thanks to Paul, and Heather and I made our way to her door.

Heather punched in the code to her penthouse, and I followed her inside.

"That was so fun," I said. "Thanks, really."

Heather kicked off her shoes, shaking her head. "You're welcome. Stop saying it."

We started out of the foyer and headed for the hallway.

"Girls?" Mrs. Fox called.

She walked into the foyer and eyed our shopping bags.

"What, Mom?" Heather asked. "We're just going to put our clothes away."

"I want to see what you got," Mrs. Fox said. She reached for Heather's bags. Heather handed over the bags.

Mrs. Fox took them to the family room and perched on the black leather couch. She only occasionally looked up at Heather. Her expression was blank, as if what she was seeing wasn't affecting her at all.

"Heather," Mrs. Fox said, brushing back a lock of stray blond hair. "I'm glad you went shopping, but what about the color scheme we'd talked about for this year?"

Heather shrugged. "I didn't see anything pink or girly that I liked. Their selection was pathetic."

I hated that Heather had to have this conversation with her mom. It was ridiculous for Mrs. Fox to want Heather to dress in clothes she didn't like. Heather wore pink at school, but she never dressed supergirly. And I was starting to get an idea why.

Mrs. Fox's eyes locked with Heather's—almost as if

she was trying to get a read on whether her daughter was lying. Finally, after what felt like a staring contest that lasted for hours, Mrs. Fox handed Heather the bags.

"I'll make sure you get proper clothes sent back to school," Mrs. Fox said.

"Thanks, Mom," Heather said. She gave what I knew was her fake smile, and I followed her out of the living room.

"Not," Heather muttered once we got into the hallway.

We went to Heather's room and laid out all of our clothes on her bed. I didn't want to say anything about what had just happened. Heather would talk to me if she wanted to.

I stared at my shirts and skirts, thinking absently about how I couldn't wait to show them to Paige. *If we ever make up,* I thought.

"Now that you have decent clothes for the week," Heather said, "we can be seen in public together. You can still borrow my stuff if you need something, but *do not* come in my room if I'm not in here."

"I won't," I said. "And thanks."

Heather looked at her phone. "Let's get out of here and go get lunch. I'm starving."

"Me too," I said. "But we just got back. Are we allowed to go out again?"

Heather grabbed her purse off the bed and headed for her door. "No one cares what we do. You'll figure that out soon."

I picked up my purse and followed Heather, wondering if it would take me till the day I went home to get used to how things worked around the Fox household.

7

SHAKE SHACK

"WHERE TO?" PAUL ASKED HEATHER AND ME after we'd buckled up in the backseat.

"The Shake Shack, please," Heather said.

"The name alone sounds awesome," I said. "What kind of restaurant is it?"

Heather glossed and then looked at me. "It'll make you feel at home because we get to eat outside and, like, don't you do that in Union?"

"Will you stop—" I started.

"I'm kidding," Heather interrupted with a grin. "I mean, you *do* eat outside, but it's a famous NYC place that you have to visit. It's in the Flatiron District at Madison Square Park and you get to see a view of something pretty cool from there."

"What?" I asked.

"You'll see."

As if Heather ever gave me any answers. I watched out the window as we headed away from Park Avenue and toward Madison Square Park. I hadn't been there with Paige, but we'd talked about going.

I watched as we passed buildings that seemed to get taller and taller as Paul got us closer to the park.

"My apartment is barely a mile away," Heather said.

"Do you ever walk here?" I asked.

Heather looked out the window, then back at me. "Sometimes. When I need to get out or whatever."

Paul pulled up to the curb. "Enjoy your lunch, ladies," he said, smiling.

"We'll be done in an hour," Heather said. "Thanks."

We got out of the car and I was almost overwhelmed by the mass of people, the smells of food, and the honks of horns.

"So we're on Twenty-third Street," Heather explained. "And sometimes I walk up and take a right to hang out at Benvenuto Café. They have the best coffee around here."

"That sounds so cool," I said.

"Plus," Heather said, "if you get the right window

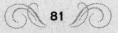

seat, you can see"——Heather turned and looked up, pointing—"that."

"Omigod, is that . . ." I paused, just staring.

"The Empire State Building."

"Wow," I breathed.

I stared at the building for a minute, not even caring that I was probably going to be run over by a stroller with three kids or knocked down by a jogger too involved in music to notice me. Heather didn't mock or sigh or yank me off the sidewalk. She let me gape at the gorgeous building until I had a mental picture I'd never forget. I hadn't been to the Flatiron District on my last trip and it was a completely new section of the city.

"Ready?" Heather asked. "They have a fun menu, but the line can be ridiculous sometimes."

I followed her into the park. Trees lined the sidewalks and plants and flowers were protected by black wire fences. It seemed odd to see so much grass and lots of trees in the middle of the city.

Heather and I got in line, about twenty people long, and waited.

"In the winter," Heather said, "if you want to eat here, the Shake Shack people turn on heaters and everyone stands under them to eat."

"Heaters?" I asked. "Whoa. That's hard-core to eat outside, when it's probably below zero in the winter on some days."

Heather nodded. "But the food here is worth it. It's not a gross street cart at the end of an alley, that no one's heard of. It's also not a pretentious, stuck-up French restaurant that my parents would much rather go to."

"So do they know you come here?" I asked.

"No. They think I come here to go to the café, which I do, but they don't know I eat burgers and hot dogs here. My mom would probably have a coronary."

"She probably would," I agreed. "But this place is so cool."

I peered around the people in front of us and looked at the "shack."

It was so awesome—I wished Canterwood would put one on campus. The giant block letters said things like CONCRETES, BURGERS, HOT DOGS. The roof slanted up, and flowers bloomed on it. I loved how the rectangular building was mostly windows, and smells of food wafted outside. There were dozens of tables and chairs, most of them filled, and people were devouring food that looked so delicious it made my stomach growl.

After only a few minutes, Heather and I were one person away from the counter.

"During the summer and typical touristy times," Heather said, "the line wraps almost around the block. We're lucky we didn't come at exactly lunchtime and that it's not a holiday."

"It's such a cool place," I said. "I get why people would want to try it if they were visiting the city."

"It's especially cool since the Flatiron Building is right over there," Heather said.

I glanced where she was looking and saw the triangular building that jutted into the sky. I'd never seen anything like it.

Heather and I moved up to the counter and I scanned the menu. Everything looked so good—I wanted to try it all!

"I'll take a ShackBurger with everything except onions, fries, and a Shack Attack," Heather said.

Ooh, the Shack Attack sounded perfect—it was all chocolate, including custard, sprinkles, chocolate chunks, and hot fudge.

"And could I have a New York Dog, fries, and a Shack Attack, too, please," I said.

The guy behind the counter nodded and rang up our

total. We handed him money from our wallets and he gave us back our change.

"That's a cool wallet," Heather said, nodding at mine. It was black with a fake diamond clasp and glitter flecks. "Macy's?"

I grinned. "Nope. H & M."

Heather stared at me for a second, then recovered. "H & M," she said slowly. "Hmm. Maybe if we have any free time, which we probably won't, we might be able to go there. Like, they might have cool accessories. Your wallet doesn't make me want to vomit, so maybe that's a good sign."

I stuffed my wallet into my purse. "Thanks. I'm glad my wallet doesn't make you want to puke."

Heather put her own Chanel wallet into her purse and we waited for our food. It didn't take long—the Shake Shack workers had it down. Within minutes we were handed our food, and we scanned the seating area.

"There's a table," I said. We walked toward it and put down our food, hanging our purses off the backs of our chairs. I took a bite of my hot dog and looked up at Heather.

"There's no way a *hot dog* can be this good," I said. "Seriously."

Heather took a giant bite of her burger and nodded. "It's weird, right? We eat burgers and hot dogs all the time at school, but there's something about the food here. I have no idea what it is."

I tried a fry, and it was just as delish as the hot dog. A sip of my chocolate milkshake cemented my idea.

"Before we go back to Canterwood," I said, "we have to load up Paul's trunk with food from Shake Shack."

Heather laughed. "I'm sure he'll appreciate that. But we could try. We'll have to get a cooler for the milkshakes."

We talked and giggled through lunch. For once, things with Heather felt easy. There wasn't any of the weirdness I'd imagined we'd have with it being just us. I'd worried about that because it hadn't really been Heather and me alone before—Julia or Alison had always been there. But without them Heather acted less like a clique leader and more like a, well, normal person.

While we ate I people-watched. There were men in suits, people in jogging clothes, women pushing strollers, a girl with a pink faux-hawk, and a guy with piercings from his earlobe to the top of his ear.

"I think a lot of people really have the wrong idea about New Yorkers," I said.

"What do you mean?" Heather asked.

"I've heard people say that New Yorkers are rude and that the city's this big, scary place. But I haven't gotten hit by a taxi or had my purse snatched."

"Yet," Heather said, smirking. "No, you're right. We get a bad rap, but I bet you could ask just about anyone on the sidewalk for directions and they'd take time to help."

"I believe it."

My phone chimed in my purse. I reached around and pulled it out.

S—can we talk soon? Pls? ~P

I snapped my phone shut and tossed it into my purse. I jammed a handful of fries into my mouth. Swallowing, I looked up at Heather. Something just made me want to talk to her. And I really didn't have anyone else.

"That was Paige," I said. "She wants to talk, but I don't have anything to say to her right now. I'm just . . ."

Heather waited, sipping her milkshake, while I tried to figure out what I was trying to say.

"I'm just stunned, I guess," I continued. "I thought we were so much closer than we were."

"Are you going to tell me what you fought about, or do we have to play that dumb guessing game that I always win?" Heather gave me The Look.

"She brought up the Jacob mess at Homecoming

dance. I have *no* idea why she did that, since I'd already told her the truth. Then she said it was more than that. I asked her what she was talking about and it just blew up. Paige said I was jealous that she had a boyfriend and I didn't."

Heather sat back in her chair. "Are you *kidding*?"

"Um, no!" I shook pepper onto my fries. "I have no clue where that came from and I told her that. I reminded her that I was the one who pushed her to get together with him."

"You'd never be jealous of Paige, especially over a boy," Heather said, her voice quiet. "I can't believe she said that."

"Me either. And that's when I told her that I wasn't staying with her over break."

"That would have been beyond uncomfortable. It was definitely the right decision to put space between you guys for a little while at least. She needs to apologize."

I took a gulp of milkshake. *Ow—brain freeze!*

"Yeah," I said, rubbing my temples. "We've had fights before, but never anything like that. I know she's sorry, but I'm not sure if she's sorry she blurted it out and meant to keep it to herself, or sorry she said that when she really didn't believe it at all."

Heather swirled a fry in ketchup. "I don't know. That's a serious thing to say to your best friend, especially after you did tell her the truth about your party. She has to know you'd never be jealous that she has a boyfriend or be worried that you'd try to steal Ryan from her. That's ridiculous."

"I know. Deep down I think Paige knows that too. But I keep seeing her face and hearing her say those words."

"Is Ryan her first boyfriend?" Heather asked.

"Yeah. She crushed on a guy back home, but she came to Canterwood before they ever had a chance at anything. Ryan is her first boyfriend, so I could get over it if she was worried about other girls, but not *me*. You know?"

"Totally," Heather said. "You guys have been disgustingly close since you came to Canterwood, and just because she gets a boyfriend, she can't suddenly be paranoid that her BFF is going to steal him or that if you're acting upset or weird it's because you're miserable without a guy in your life."

Even though Paige and I were fighting, I still didn't want Heather dissing Paige. But I didn't want to let Heather know that what she'd said had bothered me.

"And that's the thing—I'm not even looking! I have . . . feelings for Jacob, but I want to be single. I really

do. Every time I've been with a guy, things got all messed up. I'm going back to putting riding and school as my top priorities."

Heather raised her milkshake in a toast. "I second you putting riding first. My team isn't going to have any loser riders on it." She said it with a smile, though, and I laughed. I tapped my shake to hers and we finished our lunch in the warm New York air.

A half hour later Heather and I met Paul by the curb. We got into the car and he smiled at us from the rearview mirror.

"How was lunch?" he asked.

"Amazing," I said. "I wish we had a Shake Shack in Connecticut!"

Paul nodded. "Their burgers and hot dogs can't be beat. Where to, girls?"

Heather paused. "I guess we should go home." Her face had lost its earlier perkiness and she didn't sound at all excited about the idea of going to the penthouse.

"We can watch movies or something," I said.

"Yeah," Heather said. She looked a little happier at that suggestion.

Paul nodded and pulled away from the curb.

"Anyway, by the time we get back, we won't have

90

many hours to kill," Heather said. "We'll be out all day tomorrow, so that'll be something to look forward to."

"What're we doing tomorrow?" I asked.

"Going riding since we really do need to practice, and then . . ." Heather leaned closer to me. "We'll get Paul to take us on a secret mani/pedi trip. We'll just let my dad think we've been riding that whole time."

I leaned back in my seat, nodding. "That sounds awesome." I'd had a manicure only once, for a girl's birthday party back when I went to Union Middle School. It really *did* sound awesome—I just didn't want to get caught by Mr. Fox.

8

LIMITLESS

ON MONDAY MORNING MY ALARM WENT OFF at six. I grabbed my clothes, toothbrush, shampoo, body wash, and moisturizer and headed for the bathroom. I locked the door behind me and took a second to figure out how to turn on the shower faucet. The shower head was one of those superfancy ones with different massage settings. After I showered, brushed my teeth, and dried my hair, I got dressed in my best pair of fawn-colored breeches and a waffle-knit burnt orange shirt.

I put my stuff back in my room and saw the light on my phone blinking. It was a voice mail. I punched number one and waited for the message to play.

"Sasha, it's Paige. I texted you yesterday and you didn't reply. I, um, really want to talk and apologize. I know you're in the city, and maybe we could meet up and get coffee or something? Please call me."

I pushed the Delete key and tossed my phone on the bed. I walked over to one of the windows and stood there taking in the view. Sun glinted off buildings so high they looked as if they'd sway if even a slight breeze blew through the city. Below the building, cars moved slowly through the traffic and pulled in and out of the building's driveway. It made me think about home and how different my life was from Heather's.

I lived on a quiet street in the 'burbs, and my room was half the size of Heather's. But it wasn't just about the space. My house felt like, well, home. A place where people wouldn't be afraid to touch anything or break a Tiffany lamp. Heather's penthouse was gorgeous, sleek, and sophisticated, but it was cold. I wondered if it seemed that way to her, too. Or if it felt like home to her since she'd grown up here.

I turned away from the window. Suddenly I wanted to call my mom and say hi. I just needed to hear a friendly voice.

I dialed, knowing she and Dad were definitely up. They were probably planning the day from their room at the bed-and-breakfast they were staying at for vacation.

"Hi, hon!" Mom said. "How are things going?"

Just the sound of her voice made me relax. I sat at the end of the guest bed and pressed the phone to my ear.

"Really well," I said. "I'm having lots of fun. Today, Heather and I are going riding and then getting our nails done later."

I could feel Mom's smile through the phone. "That sounds wonderful, sweetie. I'm sure you'll miss riding Charm, but I bet you'll get a lot out of riding another horse."

"Mr. Conner would definitely agree with that," I said. "He always encouraged us to ride as many different horses as we can."

"How are things with Heather?" Mom asked. "Have you heard from Paige?"

I paused. I didn't want to lie about Paige, but I also didn't want to talk about it. "Heather's being very cool," I said. "We're getting along, and I haven't talked to Paige yet."

There. That was true. I hadn't said Paige had texted and called me, but it was close enough.

"Well, I'm sure you two will talk soon and you'll work out your disagreement," Mom said.

"Me too."

But I wasn't sure. When I'd called Mom the night of the dance, I'd told her Paige and I had gotten in a fight and I'd wanted to go to Heather's for break. Mom and Dad had both agreed, but they'd been sorry Paige and I hadn't been able to spend the break together that we'd planned.

"How's the B and B?" I asked, desperate to change the subject.

"It's completely charming," Mom said. "Exactly what your dad and I hoped for. It's not one of those that makes you do scheduled activities, so you're free to do what you want during your stay. Today, your dad and I are going to visit a local art museum."

"That sounds fun," I said. "I better get to breakfast, but tell Dad I said hi."

"I will, hon. Bye."

"Bye."

We hung up and I took a giant breath before walking out of my room. I walked down the hallway to Heather's room and found her on her laptop with her back to me. She was on her e-mail.

"Hey," I said.

She jumped and closed the window. "God, Silver. Don't you know to say something when you walk into a room?"

"I did," I said.

"Yeah," Heather said, shutting the lid of her Mac. "After you were breathing down my neck."

"Sorry," I said. "I'll be sure to text you next time I'm going to walk into your room."

Heather glared at me. "Ha ha."

She'd showered and dressed too. Her chocolate brown breeches contrasted with her stark white v-neck shirt.

"Let's eat and go ride," Heather said. She got out of her desk chair and I followed her out of her room.

We ate another great breakfast—I had Greek yogurt with granola, and Heather had slices of turkey bacon with scrambled eggs. We grabbed our purses, helmets, and boots and met in the foyer.

Heather's phone rang and she looked down at it, her face almost matching the color of her shirt.

"Hi, Dad," she said.

She listened for a long time, and even though I couldn't make out the words, I could hear Mr. Fox's sharp tone.

"We're going right now," Heather said. "Yes. I know. We will. Okay."

She rolled her eyes at me.

"I'll call your secretary after, promise. Bye."

Heather clicked the phone off and shoved it into her

purse. I didn't ask her about the call and she didn't offer up any information. I wasn't going to make her uncomfortable if she didn't want to talk about it. We pulled on our riding boots and I looked around the rug, checking to make sure I didn't leave mud or dirt anywhere.

Heather pulled open the door and stepped into the hallway. I followed her, glancing back behind us.

"Don't we have to tell someone we're leaving?" I asked.

Heather shook her head. "Please. Dad told Mom first thing this morning that we were going riding. She'll have someone call if she wants to know what we're doing."

"Okay."

The building was busy this morning as people hurried to work. Cars waited around the half-circle drive to pick up passengers. Heather and I stood by the curb.

"I texted Paul when I got my stuff," Heather said. "He'll be here in a sec."

And two cars later, I saw the Foxes' familiar car pull up. Paul got out and opened both doors, helping us into the backseat.

"Off to Westchester, right, Heather?" Paul asked.

"Right," Heather said. "Thanks."

We buckled up and Paul drove out of the building's driveway and up the busy streets of Manhattan.

"How far is Westchester?" I asked. "I've never been there."

"Like, less than half an hour," Heather said. "The last stable in Manhattan closed a while ago, and, besides, Westchester has a fab riding program."

I shifted one leg over the other, trying not to get nervous.

Paul navigated through the traffic, and soon we were out of the city and heading north.

"What's your old stable like? Do you still have friends there?" I asked. I needed *something* before I just walked in and started riding.

"It's called Chesterfield Stables," Heather said. "It's a lot like Canterwood, minus the school. There are three arenas—two outdoor and one indoor. I think there are fifty-something stalls, and people can board their own horses or ride school horses. Lessons are offered before and after school for students, and there are late-night sessions for adult riders."

"Wow," I said. I thought about Briar Creek, my old stable, and how it was nothing like Chesterfield. It had one outdoor arena and less than twenty stalls. It was a little run-down, but I'd loved it, and Charm and I had learned the basics there. Kim, my old instructor, had

taught me all she could until she'd encouraged me to apply to Canterwood.

"As for friends," Heather said, "yeah, I've got some there. I haven't seen them much, only if I get to Chesterfield to ride when I'm home, so I don't know if they'll be there or not."

"Maybe if your old school's on break," I said.

"Like I had time to check the calendar for a school I don't even attend," Heather said.

We both looked out the window as the car zipped along the highway.

"Will your old instructor be there?" I asked. I knew Heather would be annoyed that I kept asking questions, but I couldn't help it. I wanted to know more about the stable.

"She should be," Heather said. "Are you nervous or something?"

"Yes!" I said. "I'm going to a new stable and I'm going to be riding a different horse. Plus, there might be people from your old school there and I've never met them."

And I didn't say it, but I was secretly afraid that they were all like Heather was before we'd become friends. I just wanted to ride—not fight with mean girls.

Heather sighed, and she looked less aggravated. "Don't

worry about it. Seriously. If my friends are there, they'll be totally cool because you're with me. And my instructor will give you a good horse. When you tell her you're on the YENT, she'll know what you can handle. Trust me."

"Okay," I said, letting out a breath. I tried to concentrate on the scenery. The farther away we got from the city, the more trees and smaller towns we drove through. Some were tiny upstate New York towns with signs that said POPULATION: 2,000. They were like villages. Even Union was bigger than that.

"We're in Bedford," Paul said.

"That means we'll be at Chesterfield in, like, two minutes," Heather said.

My stomach swirled. Despite what Heather said, I was still nervous. It was my second year at Canterwood, and sometimes the fanciness of the stable still caught me off guard. I didn't want to walk into Heather's stable all wide-eyed and like I'd never been to a prestigious stable before. Mechanically I reached into my purse and pulled out the first lip gloss I could grab. Spearmint. Perfect. Hopefully the mint would somehow calm my stomach.

"Silver," Heather said. She was staring at me.

"What?" I turned to look at her.

"I said your name twice."

"Sorry," I said. "I was just thinking."

"Well, stop. When we get out, try not to do anything embarrassing, okay? Like, don't let go of a horse like you did on your first day at Canterwood."

The memory made my cheeks burn as I flashed back to my first day at Canterwood. I'd been leading Charm toward the stable when a car had backfired in the parking lot. Already antsy from the new surroundings, Charm reared and I'd been surprised. The lead line had slipped through my hands and he'd torn off across the campus. He'd headed toward the outdoor arena, where Heather and her horse, Aristocrat, had been practicing. Charm had spooked Aristocrat, and Heather had fallen off. It had been a *great* start to our relationship at Canterwood. Not.

"I won't," I said. "And bringing that up made me feel so much better—thanks."

Paul flicked on the right blinker and turned onto a gravel driveway. We drove up a steady hill and passed light brown fences that seemed to stretch on for miles. At least a dozen horses grazed in the lush pastures on either side of the driveway, and I swallowed—this *was* just like Canterwood.

The driveway leveled off and Paul pulled the car to the side of the massive stable. I couldn't move—I just stared

out the window. The glossy, seal brown stable looked as if it had been painted yesterday. Windows, trimmed in white, were everywhere. At the front, the sliding doors were open, and I peered around Heather to see inside.

"Just get out of the car," Heather hissed.

"Right," I said. I grabbed my helmet from the seat and got out as Paul opened my door.

"Have fun riding, Sasha," Paul said. He winked at me. "You'll do great."

"Thanks," I said, barely able to get out the word.

Paul let Heather out of the car. "What time should I come back?" he asked Heather.

"I'll text you about an hour before we're ready to go," Heather said. "We've got something *else* to do after this, okay?"

Paul nodded, smiling. "Understood. Don't practice too hard."

He got into the car and headed back down the drive.

Together, Heather and I stood and looked at her old stable. When I glanced over at her, I noticed she had an expression on her face that mirrored how I felt. Could it be that Heather Fox was a little intimidated by coming home?

"Let's stop standing here like idiots," Heather said, pushing back her shoulders.

She marched forward and I hurried after her. I glanced around at the arenas and saw that even on a superearly Monday morning, riders were practicing jumping and dressage in the arenas. Two older girls who looked like they were in college led stunning Dutch Warmbloods out of the stable, and Heather and I stepped over to give them room.

"Gorgeous," I breathed.

"They're all like that here," Heather said. We stepped inside the stable and I had to force myself to keep walking and not stop in the middle of the aisle. Every stall was a box stall with black iron bars over the front. Some horses had their elegant heads poked over the stall doors. I saw a hot walker toward the end of the aisle, and there were dozens of pairs of cross-ties.

"We have to go upstairs," Heather said. "That's where the offices are."

"Offices? Like, plural?"

Heather took a right and I followed her. "Yeah. There are always at least five instructors working here. Some of them go out of town to show their own horses and they might be gone for weeks. So there needs to be someone to step in. My old instructor stopped showing because of a back injury, so she's always here."

"How'd she get hurt?" I asked as we climbed a flight of stairs.

"She was riding at the Red Hills trial and her horse stopped before a log jump. She flipped over his head and cracked a few vertebrae in her back. She couldn't jump again after that—it would be too jarring on her back."

"That's awful," I said. "I can't even imagine."

"I know. And she loves teaching, but it can't be the same. I have no idea what I'd do if I ever got hurt like that."

"Me either." I shook my head, not even wanting to think about it.

We reached the top of the stairs and walked past several closed office doors to one that was half-open.

Heather knocked on the door. "Pam?"

"Come in."

Heather pushed open the door and we walked inside.

"Heather! It's so good to see you," the woman I assumed had to be Pam said, smiling.

The petite brunette with her hair in a French braid got up and hugged Heather.

"I'm glad to see you, too," Heather said. "Sorry if Dad called you, like, a zillion times before I got here."

Pam waved her hand. "Don't worry about it. I handled it.

You know how much you need to practice for Canterwood's schooling show. You don't need me to babysit you while you ride here."

"Thanks," Heather said. "And this is my . . . friend. Sasha. She's on the YENT with me."

"Nice to meet you," Pam said, shaking my hand. Her grasp was firm. "Congratulations on making the YENT. Not many do. It's incredibly competitive."

"It's nice to meet you, too," I said. "And I'm excited to be on the YENT. It's hard work, but I love it."

Pam smiled. "You sound like one of my former students." She looked at Heather.

"Sasha's ready to practice, just like I am," Heather said. "Are any horses free?"

Pam nodded. "Since your dad got in touch with me, I made sure I had two horses ready. And I think the indoor arena's empty."

"Thank you," I said. "I really appreciate you letting me ride here."

"Not a problem," Pam said. She checked a clipboard on her desk, which was as organized as Mr. Conner's. Every paper clip was in place, and manila files were stacked in neat piles.

"Your horses are in stalls eighteen and nineteen. You can

choose between yourselves which horse you'd like," Pam continued. "You know the tack-room system, Heather, but ask a groom for help if you need it."

"I will," Heather said. "Thanks. See you later."

"Bye," I said.

Pam waved us both out of her office. "Have a good session," she called after us.

Heather and I went down the stairs and she headed away from the aisle.

"Let's grab our tack," Heather said.

We walked a few yards down a side aisle that was lit from skylights. The walls were lined with championship ribbons—some from show circuits I'd never even heard of. Heather turned a brass knob on a closed door. The scent of leather and saddle soap felt immediately comforting. There were racks of saddles, bridles, and saddle pads all around the room. Every saddle was so shiny, I half-expected to see my reflection if I looked at one up close.

"This tack room is amazing," I said. "Do the grooms clean the saddles after every ride or something? They're all so perfect."

"They don't have time to do that," Heather said, shrugging. "They just get a lot of use, so they never get dusty. And they're so expensive, I'm sure their riders clean them

every few rides." She walked down the row and pointed. "Here's our tack." I looked closer and saw the saddle racks had golden plates with numbers inscribed on them.

I lifted the Stübben all-purpose saddle and white saddle pad from the rack and looped the bridle over my arm. The snaffle bit gleamed—every inch of leather was supple and polished. Heather gathered her own tack and we left the tack room. The aisle was quiet, but the riders who were here looked like adults or college students. Most of the people our age were probably still in school—not everyone got fall break like we did.

If my arms hadn't been full of tack, I would have petted every horse in sight. These were some of the most gorgeous horses I'd ever seen. Not as handsome as Charm, of course. Just thinking about my chestnut Thoroughbred/Belgian gelding made my heart twist. I missed him so much. I knew Mike and Doug, my favorite Canterwood grooms, were taking excellent care of Charm, but I still worried about how he was doing without me. We were only apart on school breaks, and he followed me like a puppy whenever I got back to school.

Heather and I reached stalls eighteen and nineteen and put the tack down on the trunks in front of the stalls.

"Do you know these horses?" I asked, peering into

stall eighteen. The nameplate said LIMITLESS. Inside, a lanky bay gelding with a star on his forehead munched on hay from the iron rack on the wall. He looked up at me and his dark brown eyes were friendly.

The horse in stall nineteen, a black mare, had her head poked over the door and stretched her muzzle toward Heather. Her nameplate said CORA.

"They're new," Heather said. "I didn't see either of them when I was here last time."

"Which one do you want?" I asked. It seemed only polite to let Heather have first choice since it was her old stable.

"The mare's fine," Heather said. "Cool?"

I nodded. "Totally."

I took the lead line off the hook by Limitless's stall and unlatched his stall door.

"Hi, boy," I said. I held out my hand and walked toward him, placing a hand on his shoulder.

He turned his head away from the hay net and sniffed my arm. I clipped the lead line to the ring under his chin and rubbed his neck.

"I'm Sasha," I said, keeping my voice low. Heather would mock me for days if she heard me introducing myself to a horse.

"Pam said I can ride you this week," I said. "It's important, since I'm practicing for a schooling show when I get
back to my stable," I added. "Ready to go for a ride?"

Limitless's eyes met mine and he looked ready. I petted
his neck for a few more seconds, thinking about what it
must be like to be a school horse. Different riders at least
every week. Each rider had his or her own style of riding,
and school horses didn't know what to expect and had to
adapt to every new rider.

I led Limitless out of the stall, grabbed his tack box from
his trunk, and found a pair of cross-ties a few stalls down.
Cora walked obediently behind Heather as they followed
Limitless and me. Heather tied Cora to the bars of an empty
stall nearby so we could chat while we groomed them.

"Are you freaking out about riding here?" Heather
asked.

"Not anymore," I said. "Pam was so nice and welcoming. Plus it seems like we'll have the indoor arena to
ourselves."

"Good," Heather said. "Because I want to practice
hard. We've got the schooling show coming up and I'm
not going to my first show on the YENT unprepared.
You never know who might be at that circuit and we can't
look like losers."

I picked up the dandy brush and looked at Heather. "You don't mean . . ."

Heather ducked under Cora's neck to look at me. "You never know. Just because she's not showing for the YENT doesn't meant she can't be there competing at a different level."

I took a long breath. Neither of us had said her name, but we both knew the girl we were talking about—Jasmine King. Jas, an ultracompetitive rider, had transferred from her school—Wellington Preparatory—to Canterwood last semester. The girl was so mean she made Heather look angelic. But Jas had gone too far when she'd framed Julia and Alison for cheating on a history exam. They'd been kicked off the advanced riding team and hadn't been given a shot at trying out for the YENT. We'd brainstormed ways to prove their innocence but had come up empty. Finally I'd caught Jas on tape bragging about how she'd framed them. It had been proof enough of Julia's and Alison's innocence. They were back on Canterwood's advanced riding team and would soon be able to try out for the YENT.

I realized I was just standing there—not brushing Limitless. I pushed Jasmine out of my head and started brushing. Jasmine wasn't at Canterwood anymore. She wasn't on the YENT, and there was nothing she could do to mess with Charm and me. There were other important things to focus on—like the schooling show.

A few minutes later, I switched to a softer blue body brush and ran it across Limitless's neck and back, flicking nonexistent dust from his coat. Chestnuts were my favorite, but I loved how bays shined. Beside me, Heather worked silently, seemingly caught up in her own thoughts.

"Does it feel weird to be back here?" I asked. I took a soft cloth and wiped Limitless's face.

Heather shrugged. "Kind of. It's weird coming back to a stable that used to be *yours* and to have people and horses you've never met be here."

"That's how I felt when I visited Briar Creek, my old stable, after being at Canterwood," I said. "It was strange to see my old instructor working with students I'd never met and not to have Charm in his old stall."

"Your stable wasn't anything like this, was it?"

Heather had *never* asked about Briar Creek. She'd mocked Union, my hometown, and had known that I'd come from a tiny stable without a reputation like Canterwood's. But she hadn't ever talked to me about Briar Creek's facilities.

"No, it wasn't," I said, deciding to be completely honest.

"Our outdoor arena was more like a round pen with peeling paint. There were only a handful of stalls and not too many boarders. But Kim, my old instructor, kept it as clean as Canterwood and did what she could with repairs."

Heather nodded and started to saddle Cora. "Did Kim teach you the basics?"

"Yeah, but she knew Briar Creek couldn't give me what I needed to keep progressing. She encouraged my parents to help me apply to Canterwood and I did." I paused, thinking about the bittersweet moment when I'd heard I'd been accepted.

"It was weird, you know?" I said. "I loved Briar Creek and I was comfortable there. It was like my second home. Canterwood sounded so scary and intimidating. But I knew if I didn't take the chance, I wouldn't grow as a rider. So I took it."

I walked a few feet away to grab Limitless's saddle and pad. I smoothed the pad onto his back and placed the saddle over it. He stood still while I tightened his girth and ran my hand under it, making sure none of his skin was pinched.

I released the cross-ties and slid the reins over Limitless's head. I put the bit on my palm and he opened his mouth without hesitation.

"You're such a good guy," I said. "You're used to having this done a lot, aren't you?"

He mouthed the bit until it was settled, and I tightened the cheek strap.

Heather had finished tacking up Cora.

"Ready?" she asked.

"Definitely," I said. We grabbed our helmets off the tack trunks, and I followed her toward the indoor arena.

9

YOU LOOK LIKE
A BIRD

WHEN WE REACHED THE ARENA, I STOPPED at the entrance, taking it all in. It was a gorgeous space—the entire rectangular arena was flooded with light from the huge windows. A stack of portable jumps were at one end, next to a neat pile of dressage markers. The arena was almost as big as Canterwood's. It was empty—I suspected Mr. Fox had probably reserved it for the entire day.

"Niiice," I said. "This is a great space."

"I love the windows," Heather said. "It always kept me from getting bored when I was riding for hours by myself. I'd pass a window and watch someone else practice in one of the outdoor arenas."

I patted Limitless's neck and prepared to mount. It

had been a while since I'd ridden another horse, but I wasn't too nervous. Pam seemed to know what Heather and I could handle, especially since we were on the YENT. Gathering the reins, I stuck my left toe in the stirrup iron and pushed up off the ground.

Limitless didn't move as I settled into the saddle and reached down to adjust my stirrups. Beside us Heather mounted Cora, and the black mare pointed her ears toward the arena—definitely ready to go.

Heather and I gave the horses rein and let them move at a slow walk through the arena entrance. I guided Limitless to the wall, and, with Heather and Cora behind us, we started to warm up. Limitless's stride was smooth and he was alert and ready for any of my commands, which was great for a school horse. I flashed back to some of the horses I'd ridden before my parents had bought me Charm. They'd been an interesting mix. The first lesson horse I'd ridden had refused to trot unless he wanted to and he'd always yanked his head down to try and grab a bite of grass. A couple of horses had been high-strung and one had shied at anything that moved.

But Limitless wasn't anything like those horses, and from what I'd seen from Cora, she wasn't either. I gave the bay gelding more rein and let him move into a trot.

He quickened his pace and moved smoothly around the arena. Hoofbeats quickened behind us as Heather let Cora trot after Limitless. The mare didn't want to be left behind, and she stayed a few strides behind us without tailgating.

As we made our way around the arena, I looked out one of the windows. In the arena that was in full view, half a dozen adult riders were putting horses through all different exercises. I was so used to seeing people my age in the arena that I almost wanted to stop and watch the adults ride.

"Silver!" Heather yelled from behind me.

"What?" I looked over at her as she let Cora get even with Limitless.

"I know I said the windows were great, but you can't stare out them forever," Heather continued. "We're supposed to be *practicing*."

"We're just warming up. And chill—I might learn something from watching them."

Heather rolled her eyes. "The warm-up's about to be over and the only person you'd learn anything from watching is me." She shifted in the saddle to look at me, a cocky smirk on her face.

"Omigod," I said, laughing. "Did you really just say that?"

Heather stared at me as if my helmet was on fire or something.

Heather let Cora into a canter, and the mare jumped in front of Limitless, swishing her tail. She was lanky, and her long legs carried her strides ahead of us. I stopped posting and sat in the saddle, giving Limitless rein and squeezing my legs against his sides. He transitioned from a trot to a canter in a few strides, and his canter was smooth enough that I had no trouble not bouncing in the saddle.

We followed Cora and Heather around the arena twice at a canter before Heather eased her to a trot and guided her into the center of the arena.

I pulled Limitless to a trot, then a walk, before stopping him next to Cora.

"I assume you already have our entire workout planned," I said.

Heather nodded. "Down to the cooldown."

I looked at her, waiting. "I'm ready. Let's go instead of just sitting here."

That made Heather smile. "Exactly what I wanted to hear. Let's start by going through flatwork without stirrups, and after that, we'll use the stirrups to work through a little dressage, and then give the horses a break for a few minutes."

"Oh, yeah, we'll totally be giving the *horses* a break," I said.

Heather waved a hand at me. "Puh-lease. You better not need a break by then or the rest of the workout is going to kill you."

I straightened in Limitless's saddle. "As if. I'm ready, as I said, like, an hour ago."

"Fine. Drop 'em," Heather said, her eyes locked on mine.

She kicked her feet out of the stirrups and I did the same. We crossed them over our saddles and I adjusted my legs to the right position.

"I'll give directions first, then you can," Heather said. Cora pointed her ears forward and struck the ground with a foreleg. Her energy seemed to feed into Limitless, and he shifted beneath me, ready for whatever instruction I gave him.

"Deal."

"Walk to the wall, then sitting trot," Heather instructed. "And whoever is giving instructions has to ride behind the other rider and offer suggestions."

I knew what *that* meant. Suggestions meaning "you're-the-worst-rider-ever-and-do-it-right-before-I-punch-you." That's what Heather meant by "suggestions."

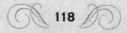

But I let her and Cora drop behind Limitless and me. I gripped the saddle gently with my knees, wanting to keep Limitless's pace steady and to keep my position in the saddle.

"Your heels are ridiculous," Heather said. "Basics 101, hello."

"They are n—" I started to argue, but I looked down and saw she was right.

My face burned a little as I pushed my heels down and pointed my toes up. That *was* a beginner mistake. Something I'd learned not to do years ago.

I felt my shoulders tense at the thought of Heather behind me, watching me and ready to jump on the next mistake. My shoulders started to inch up, and just as I caught it, Heather called, "Shoulders. Down."

I dropped them and straightened my back, trying not to look too stiff. *Stop it,* I told myself. *You've practiced with Heather before. If you're nervous all day about riding in front of her, then the entire lesson's going to be a waste. Just relax.*

And as I looked through Limitless's ears, I reminded myself that I was lucky to have a good horse too.

Heather and I made two more circuits around the arena at a sitting trot and she had no comments on those rounds.

"Walk for half a lap, and then posting trot," Heather said.

I took back a bit of rein and slowed Limitless to a walk. He listened immediately and I relaxed in the saddle, trying not to be obvious to Heather. Sitting to a trot without stirrups was hard!

All too soon we reached the halfway point and it was time to trot again. I gripped the saddle a little tighter with my knees, preparing to post. Limitless shook his black mane as I let him back into a trot, and I couldn't help smiling. He was having fun.

I moved up and down slightly with his trot and felt sweat on my forehead. But I was *not* going to let Heather see that.

"Tuck in your elbows," she called. "You look like a bird trying to take off."

I pulled my elbows closer to my sides. "Can you critique me without the side comments?"

"I guess," Heather said after a few seconds. "I don't want to distract you more than you already are."

"Right. Thanks," I said, my tone a little sharp. But we both knew she wasn't stopping just because she wanted to make my riding better for the team. There was no one else here and she didn't have to act like the old Heather Fox to keep up her image.

I focused on my posture, determined not to make a mistake for Heather to spot, and ignored the pain in my legs. Limitless kept an even pace and stuck close to the wall as if he didn't even need me to tell him what to do.

"Walk," Heather said after what felt like an eternity.

I let Limitless trot for a few more seconds, just to prove to Heather that I was fine, before I eased him to a walk.

"Good job, boy," I said, rubbing his dark brown neck. He flicked an ear back at me and snorted, seeming to know I was praising him.

Heather rode up beside me. "Not awful," she said. "I mean, once I knocked the basic beginner mistakes out of you and all."

"Gee, thanks," I said. "I'm glad I'm not 'awful.'"

But we grinned at each other.

"Do you like Cora?" I asked, letting my legs dangle at Limitless's sides.

Heather patted Cora's shoulder. "Yeah, she's great so far. But I—"

"—miss Canterwood," we both said at the same time.

Heather gave me a half smile.

"Limitless is great, but I miss Charm so much already," I said. "I can't stop wondering what he's doing right now."

"I thought about Aristocrat when I got here," Heather said. "For a second, when I walked down the aisle, I thought I heard him. But that was dumb."

"It's not dumb. You're used to seeing him every day. By the middle of the week, I'll probably be calling Mike and having him put his phone next to Charm's ear so I can tell him hi."

"Oh, God," Heather said. "That's too pathetic—even for you."

But there wasn't venom in her voice. Her eyes were teasing.

I laughed. "Okay, okay. I probably *won't* do that. But you know what I mean. I miss Charm, even though I know it's good to ride other horses."

"I miss Aristocrat too. He'll always be my favorite, but I agree—we have to ride different horses." Heather stretched her back. "Actually, I'm hoping to get another horse when I start high school so that I'll have a new one to train for the future and a more experienced horse like Aristocrat to compete with through high school."

I sat still in the saddle, just staring at Heather. "Wow. I haven't even thought that far ahead. I'm just focused on the YENT and prepping for our first schooling show. Riding in high school seems so far away."

"It's not, really," Heather said. "Not when you're going to start looking for a new horse and figuring out how to split your time between two horses."

Charm was enough for me to handle; I couldn't even imagine having another horse to ride and train.

"You look like your brain is about explode," Heather said. "Let's get back to work."

Heather guided Cora in front of Limitless, and I focused my attention on her, ready to critique.

10

GOING LUXE

"I THINK WE SHOULD STOP," HEATHER SAID. "The horses are probably tired."

Limitless seemed fine and there was barely a layer of sweat on his coat, but I wasn't about to argue with her. I was exhausted.

"Yeah, let's start cooling them down," I said. "We've got all week to practice."

I halted Limitless and dismounted, hopping to the ground. I loosened his girth and reached for the reins to pull them over his head. Heather pulled her phone out of her zipper pocket and texted whom I assumed was Paul, to tell him we'd be done after we took care of our horses.

"Heather! Omigod!"

Heather and I both turned toward the arena entrance

as two girls led horses into the arena. The girls were dressed in black breeches and polo shirts. They carried helmets under their arms. There was something so familiar about them, down to the way they walked.

"Blake! Emma! Hey!" Heather said. She led Cora over to the girls and they air-kissed.

That was it. They were Heather's friends. Part of her crowd. That's why they seemed familiar. They had Heather's confident walk, her cool gaze, and riding clothes that cost more than my summer clothing allowance. I took a breath and forced myself to meet their gaze and not look intimidated.

"Sasha," Heather said, "these are my friends from my old school."

"Blake," said a girl with long, glossy black hair. She held the reins of a steely gray gelding.

"I'm Emma," said the other girl. She had an auburn pixie cut and freckles sprinkled across her nose. Her horse, also a gelding, was a bay like Limitless, but he had a stripe.

"How are you guys?" Heather asked. "I haven't seen you on IM since forever."

"We've been *so* busy," Blake said. "You know how it is at school. Like, I'm juggling riding, classes, dating Nick, and—"

"You're dating someone?" Heather asked. "Since when? And who's Nick?"

Blake sighed. "I started dating Nick at the beginning of the year, and he's a transfer student. Didn't anyone tell you that?"

Heather shook her head. "Someone probably texted me and I just didn't get the message. My phone was broken for a while."

"Whatev," Emma said. "So Blake's with Nick, and I think Sam's about to ask me out. You remember Sam Murdock, right?"

Heather nodded. "Yeah, of course I do."

But something in her tone made me doubt her a little.

"Well," Emma continued. "We were out with a group getting sushi together and Sam couldn't stop talking to me. His little sister is a year younger than me, so I'm totally going to get the dirt on Sam from her."

"Sound like a good plan," Heather said, her voice sounding a bit bored. "Have you guys heard any Canterwood gossip?"

Blake and Emma looked at each other.

"No," Blake said. "There must not be anything going on or we would have heard about it."

"Actually," Heather said. "We had a huge scandal when—"

She shut her mouth and her eyes narrowed when she watched Blake check the time on a dainty silver wristwatch.

"We want to catch up and tell you everything about school, but we've got to ride first," Blake said. "Looks like you and Sarah are done."

"It's Sasha," I said.

"Yeah, we're done," Heather said. "And we've got to go, anyway."

Blake nodded. "Totally. We'll text you later so we can go out or something."

"Cool," Heather said.

And with fake smiles to Emma and Blake, Heather led Cora away from them and out of the arena. I led Limitless out behind them and caught up to Heather when we reached the aisle.

"Let's cool them outside," she said. "It got a little crowded in there."

We exited the stable and headed away from the busy arenas and toward a quiet, well-worn path that took us away from the stable.

I waited until we'd walked for a couple of minutes before I got up the guts to ask what I was thinking.

"Were Emma and Blake your best friends at your old school?" I asked.

"Yeah." Heather shrugged. "I transferred to Canterwood a year before you, but I always stayed in touch with them. On every break I stayed at one of their apartments and we talked every day on the phone. In seventh grade . . . I don't know what happened, really. We just stopped talking so much."

"That happens sometimes," I said. "But they seemed happy to see you."

"Yeah, so happy that all they wanted to do was talk about themselves," Heather said. "They didn't ask me *anything* about what was going on at school or if *I* was dating anybody."

Heather looked over at me. "Honestly, it was annoying, but I really don't care," she said. "Julia and Alison have been my best friends for a long time and I'm not part of Emma and Blake's crowd anymore. They could have at least pretended to care what I was doing. But why, I guess? We're all going to go back to our own schools and stables and not talk anymore, anyway. I just wish I could have said . . ." Heather shook her head and pulled Cora a step in front of Limitless.

"Said what?" I asked.

I caught up with her.

"I don't know. I guess I just wish I could have said that

I was dating someone too. Not so they could go back to school and be like, 'Omigod, Heather's dating this guy from Canterwood,' but just because I want to be, you know, dating."

"Let's get specific," I said. We guided the horses down a gentle incline and reached a shallow creek. "You want to be dating Troy."

Heather paused, then nodded. "Duh, I told you I liked him at the Homecoming dance."

We gave our horses rein to take tiny sips of water from the creek.

"So what are you going to do about it?" I asked.

Heather whipped her head around to look at me. "I don't know! Nothing right now. If he's interested, he'll come talk to me."

"Please," I said. "That's so yesterday. If you want to go out with Troy, talk to him. You could text him or e-mail him over break just to say hi. Be totally casual. Or write on his FaceSpace wall or something."

Heather pulled Cora's head up from the creek, and water dribbled from the mare's muzzle. Limitless raised his head, and the two sniffed muzzles.

"No. Way," Heather said. "And we're done talking about this now. Let's get them groomed so we can go."

"Okay," I said, deciding not to argue.

We led the horses away from the sandy creek bed and back down the dirt path. But I wasn't going to give up. Heather deserved to have something in her life besides riding, and if she wanted to date Troy, she had to at least try to make it happen. She'd encouraged me the night of the dance to go after Jacob—even though I wasn't ready and had refused. Interesting that confident, I-always-get-what-I-want Heather Fox was at a surprising loss at how to handle boys. Even though my track record wasn't that great, I was sure I could help her at least start talking to Troy.

We led the horses back toward the stable in silence. Limitless kept his head close to my shoulder as we walked and I liked him more every minute I spent time with him. I reached up and rubbed his star.

On the way back to our cross-ties, Heather grabbed a bottle of kiwi-strawberry Snapple out of the fridge and took a long sip. She offered the bottle to me. I took a drink and handed it back to her.

"Thanks," I said.

We untacked the horses, and the grooms came and took the tack from us.

I brushed dried sweat off Limitless's coat with the

dandy brush and took extra care to make sure he was totally cool and clean. I ran my hand down his left foreleg and he immediately lifted his leg. He didn't lean against me like some horses did while I picked his hooves. I ran a dry cloth across his bay coat and made sure he had the same sheen as when I'd found him in his stall. I ran a comb through his mane and tail and stepped back to look at him.

"You're such a gorgeous guy," I said to him. He bobbed his head and it made me laugh—that was something Charm would do. He always knew when I complimented him. I hugged Limitless and took in the scent of hay and the sweet horse smell. "Thanks for being so good today, boy."

"Are you *still* talking to your horse?" Heather asked. She raised an eyebrow. "It's definitely time to leave. Put Limitless away and let's go. Paul should be here any second, if he's not already outside."

I unclipped him from the cross-ties and led him to his stall. I rubbed his neck again. "See you soon," I whispered.

I left him munching hay and I slid the bolt closed on his stall door.

Heather and I washed our hands and brushed our hair in the bathroom, then we left the stable and walked out to

the gravel driveway. Paul was indeed already waiting for us, and he got out of the car as soon as he saw us approaching.

"Hi, girls," he said. He opened the door and Heather got inside. I walked around to the other side of the car and stopped for Paul, still feeling awkward at waiting for someone to let me into the car. I could open the door myself! But I knew it would just irritate Heather if I didn't let Paul do his job, so I stood until he let me into the car.

I slid into the comfy seat, letting out a sigh.

Heather looked over at me with a coy smile. "Too much for you, Silver?"

"No way," I said. "That was a happy sigh. We had a great practice. I can't wait to do it again."

"Uh-huh," Heather said, not sounding at all as if she believed me.

"How was your lesson?" Paul asked as he buckled his seat belt.

"Great," Heather said. "We actually kind of challenged each other, and we definitely got a lot done."

"I'm glad to hear that," Paul said. "Now where can I take you ladies?"

"Luxe Nail Salon," Heather said. "But we were never there, okay? We've been at the stable this entire time."

Paul smiled at us in the rearview mirror. "Of course you were." He didn't question us at all as he drove down Chesterfield's driveway and back toward Manhattan.

I looked down at my ragged nails, which were gross and had dirt under them from spending the day at the stable.

Heather and I were quiet on the ride back to Manhattan. There wasn't much traffic and it took just under an hour to reach the city. Paul must have taken Heather or Mrs. Fox to the Luxe Nail Salon a lot because he knew exactly where to go—no GPS directions needed.

We pulled up to the curb and Paul turned around to face us. "I'll be back in about an hour and a half," he said. "Okay?"

"Totally," Heather said. "Thanks, Paul."

I smiled at him and got out of the car behind Heather. The nail salon was adorable. The overhang was bright pink, and the entire place was done up in pink and white. Heather walked up to the counter, and the woman behind it looked up, smiling at her.

"I'm Heather Fox," she said. "We need two mani/pedis. My mother has a credit card on file here, so please charge it to her account."

"Of course, Miss Fox," said the woman. "We have two open chairs, so if you both would choose your

colors and go to the last two seats at the end, we'll get started."

"Won't your mom see the credit card bill and know we were here?" I asked.

"She never checks that stuff," Heather said. "And even if she did, we'd be back at school by the time she noticed."

If Heather wasn't going to worry about it, I wouldn't either.

Heather and I walked over to shelves of nail polishes. I'd never seen so many.

"I have nooo idea what color to get," I said. "They're all so pretty!"

Heather's gaze was locked on the red section. "I need a power color," she said. She picked up two different reds. "Which one?"

One was slightly pink, so I point to the cherry-colored one. "Definitely that one."

"Agreed," she said.

"You should get something chic," she said. "You're in the city. Get your nails cut supershort and do a dark brown or a black. If you did black, you could coat it with a light glitter."

"Oooh, that sounds fun," I said.

I selected OPI's Black Onyx and a sheer, glittery

shade to go over it. We passed women relaxing in the pedicure massage chairs, reading *US Weekly* or *The New Yorker*. Heather and I sat down in our chairs, pulled off our boots and socks then rolled our breeches up to our knees.

I looked at my stubbly legs and wished I'd shaved last night. Ooops.

Two manicurists slid into the rolling stools in front of us and ran water in the basins in front of us. They added an emerald green liquid that smelled *so* good—like eucalyptus.

"Test the water to see if it's too hot," my manicurist said. I dipped my foot in the water, then stuck both feet in.

"It's perfect, thank you," I said.

She turned on jet bubbles and pulled down my armrests. "Here's your massage controller."

While my feet soaked, I played with my massage controller. It was like an oversize TV remote with buttons that lit up in orange when I pushed them. I could have my lower back kneaded, pounded, or rolled. There was even a button to slide the massager up and down my back, neck, and shoulders depending on where I wanted it. Another button to turned the heat on and off. I closed my eyes as it

eased the tension from my neck and worked its way down to my lower back.

I peeked over at Heather and saw that her head was tilted back as the massage chair worked its magic on her.

A few minutes later our manicurists reappeared, and mine lifted my right foot out of the water and removed my old nail polish.

"Cut or just file?" she asked.

"File, please," I said.

She got to work on my toenails, and once they were shaped, she rubbed my feet and lower legs with a scrub that smelled like vanilla. Lotion was next and I could feel how soft my feet were without even touching them. She slipped my feet into cozy flip-flops and wound cotton between my toes. Nail polish remover wiped any lotion off my nails, and then she applied two coats of the black polish.

"Nice," Heather said, looking over.

"Thanks." I glanced over at her toes. They were a gorgeous red. "Yours look so pretty. The color looks great."

Heather glanced at her own toes and nodded. "Good choice, Silver."

Once a coat of shimmer was applied to my toenails, the manicurist helped me out of the massage chair and took Heather and me to two side-by-side, pretty pink tables for our manicures.

The manicurist repeated on my nails the process she'd just done on my toes. She knew just how short to make them to make the black polish look cool instead of scary.

After our nails were painted, the manicurists led Heather and me to the dryers. They turned them on, and our toes and fingers were blasted with heat and a UV light. While our nails dried, the manicurists massaged our backs and necks.

I wanted to live here. Or at least get a mani/pedi here every day.

"Thank you, girls," they said as they finished our massages. "Please come again."

"Thank you," Heather and I said.

"I always dry for two cycles," Heather said. "Otherwise, your nails might smudge."

I nodded, not wanting mine to smudge. Any chips or smudges would be especially visible with the black polish.

We sat through two drying cycles and then tested our nails.

"Mine are dry," I said.

"Mine too," Heather said.

We put our boots back on and waved at the manicurists on the way out.

"Thanks!" I said.

They smiled at us and we went to the curb to wait for Paul.

"Um, I just thought of this, but won't your mom notice that we got our nails done?" I asked.

"No way," Heather said. "She only talks to me when she has to, and even then she's not really looking at me. There's no way she'll notice our nails. Trust me. I'll tell her we just got back from riding, which we really kind of did, and that'll be it."

"Okay," I said. But I couldn't help worrying just a little. I didn't want either of us to get in trouble.

I glanced around, not sure what part of the city we were in.

"We're just a few blocks away from my apartment," Heather said, answering my unspoken question. "Stop glancing around like you're lost."

I kept my head still, but my eyes roamed over the street. Traffic flowed up and down—a never-ending stream of cars. People moved at a steady pace along the sidewalks, able to somehow text or talk on a BlackBerry and carry a giant Starbucks cup while not running into anyone. I

definitely wasn't a New Yorker yet—if I tried that, I'd spill coffee all over myself and whomever I bumped into.

"There's Paul," Heather said. She looked down the street and we watched as he pulled up to the curb. We got into the car, and the ride to the penthouse seemed to take seconds instead of minutes.

We took the elevator, walked down the hallway, and Heather let us into the apartment. We tugged off our boots and I stretched my arms.

"I'm going to take a shower," I said. I was gross from the stable.

"Me too," Heather said.

We headed toward the hallway and almost smacked into Mr. Fox.

"Dad," Heather said. There was surprise in her voice. "You're home early."

She said the second sentence much more calmly. I wanted to jam my newly manicured hands into my pockets, but my breeches didn't have any. *Calm down,* I told myself. *It's not likely that Mr. Fox is looking at your nails.*

"I left paperwork here," Mr. Fox said. "I'm going back to work in a few minutes." He looked so intimidating in his black suit, stark white shirt, and red tie.

"Okay. See you later," Heather said.

Yes! Made it! I thought.

"Wait a minute," Mr. Fox said. "I want to hear about your practice session. Pam was supposed to have the indoor arena reserved, and two of her best horses were to be available."

"We had the arena to ourselves, and Sasha and I got perfect horses," Heather said. "We worked through a solid warm-up, and then ran through flatwork and jumping. We coached each other and neither of us held back on our critiques."

Mr. Fox glanced at me. "Is it enough for you, Heather, to have another competitor critiquing you? Or do you need Pam or another instructor to oversee lessons for the rest of the week?"

"We're fine, Dad," Heather said. Tension was inching into her voice. "We're both on the same team and it wouldn't benefit either of us to work against the other."

Mr. Fox stared at both of us for several looong seconds before he nodded. "All right. But I don't want any reports from Mr. Conner when you return to school that your riding is not up to par. Understood?"

Mr. Fox was speaking to Heather, but I found myself nodding along with her.

"Okay, Dad," Heather said.

Mr. Fox stepped around us and headed for the door.

Blowing out a breath of relief, I followed Heather down the hallway, and without saying a word, we went to our rooms.

11

SUGAR HIGH

AFTER BREAKFAST ON TUESDAY MORNING Heather pushed back her chair and motioned for me to get up.

"What?" I asked.

"We're not going riding today. My parents already left, so they'll never know."

"Are you sure?" I asked. "I don't want to get caught."

Heather smoothed her royal purple v-neck tee. "We won't get in trouble. Relax. Since you're here with a *real* New Yorker, I thought you needed to see the best parts of the city."

I opened my mouth to defend Paige, since Heather knew I'd stayed in the city with her and Paige was a "real New Yorker" too, but I stopped myself.

"That sounds really fun," I said. "It'll be cool to have you show me around. Thanks."

Heather snorted. "Please. Don't get all soap opera-y on me. I just don't want to go riding, and all of the places I'm taking you are spots I haven't been to in a while and have wanted to visit."

"Okay," I said. "Let me grab my purse."

"And not that you would," Heather called after me, "but don't wear heels. You're going to want comfortable shoes to walk around in."

I didn't bother responding to her comment. Instead I walked into the guest room and grabbed my black flip-flops and my purse. I passed the full-length mirror and checked my reflection. If we were going out in the city, I wanted to look good. Maybe I'd run into a celebrity!

My dark-wash jeans looked good with my pale pink keyhole top. I'd straightened my hair this morning, and so far it hadn't gotten wavy. The tiny amount of makeup I'd applied earlier—concealer, mascara, and blush—was still in place.

I grabbed my purse off the bed and reached for my phone on the nightstand.

The red light was blinking, which meant I had a message. I flipped open my phone and saw ONE NEW TEXT.

I opened the message. *Sasha, I'm so, so sry. Pls call me? Or txt me. I just want to talk. ~Paige*

I stared at the message for a few seconds before I deleted it and shoved my phone into my purse. Heather and I were going out exploring today—I didn't have time to call or text Paige back right now.

When we got into the waiting car, Paul already seemed to know where to go.

"So are you going to tell me where we're going or are you going to blindfold me till we get there?" I asked.

"Knew I forgot something," Heather said. "Whatev, I'll tell you. We're going to Rockefeller Center," Heather said. "Did you go there with Paige?"

"Uh, no," I said, caught off guard. "We meant to, but we didn't have time."

"Good. Then you'll get to see it right. It's always busy, but it shouldn't be ridiculous with a zillion people, like it is during the holidays."

"That would be annoying."

"It *is*. The tourists take pictures of everything, and you can't move. Police try to direct them across the streets because they don't understand how the street signs work, but you always hear on the news about someone getting hit by a taxi or something."

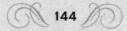

"Whoa," I said. "Now I'm definitely glad it's not Christmas or anything."

Heather nodded. "I mean, the tree and the lights are gorgeous, but it's just a mass of swarming people. Ugh." She grinned. "I think every New Yorker who has to work near Rock Center probably throws a party when the holidays *end*."

I laughed. "Probably. They're taking back their city."

It took Paul less than ten minutes to reach Rock Center. "We're going to walk around for a while," Heather said. "I want to show Sasha a bunch of shops and stuff. Can you meet us back here in a couple of hours?"

Paul nodded. "Sure thing. Be safe and call me if you need anything."

Heather got out of the car and I followed her. I looked up and saw NBC's Today Show studio. The actual studio I saw on TV! The walls were glass, and a giant ticker with red letters scrolled the latest headline news. Heather and I walked closer and stopped, peering through the glass. Inside they were filming and I recognized one of my favorite anchors.

"This is so cool!" I said. It looked *so* different on TV. The actual studio was filled with hundreds of carefully positioned lights, and a maze of wires was taped to the

floor. Heather and I watched as the anchors discussed the morning's news and read their lines from giant cue cards and a teleprompter.

"It's kind of surreal to see people you watch on TV in person," Heather said. "The first time I walked by the studio, it was *nothing* like I expected. I guess I only thought I'd see the set I was used to seeing from my TV screen. I didn't think about the camera crew, sound guys, and all of the lighting."

"I definitely didn't expect to see any of that," I said.

We left the Today Show studio and Heather pointed down over a railing. "That's where the ice rink is set up for the winter. It'll probably open in a month or two, depending on the weather."

I looked around at the various statues that were placed around the space. There were so many things to look at—it was almost dizzying.

"You have to see the concourse next," Heather said.

"What's that?" I asked.

"You'll see," Heather said.

Heather and I walked through a light crowd and took steps downstairs.

"So there are a bunch of subway train lines down here—not that I'd use them," Heather said. "We're at

Forty-seventh Street at Rock Center. But if you don't keep going downstairs to the trains, it's beyond awesome."

We stopped in front of ATM machines and Heather pointed. "There's a book publisher that way. But if we go left, we'll start hitting the shops."

"I'm just stuck on the fact that there's an underground shopping center," I said. "This would be the place to shop and eat during gross days."

"Definitely," Heather said.

We walked past a Starbucks with a Subway across from it. A few policemen patrolled the area, and as soon as we got away from the subway entrances and exits, it got quieter. And as we kept walking, I almost couldn't believe something this cool existed underground. It felt like one of those things you'd want to keep secret and not tell anyone else about.

"Back there," Heather said, pointing, "are banks and a few other businesses."

We entered another section of the concourse. In front of us was a Hallmark store that looked packed. Maybe everyone was getting cards to send home to share details about their NYC trip.

And the stores were endless. We passed a vitamin store, a drugstore, and at least a dozen restaurants. One looked particularly cool—it was called Just Salad and the people in line gave instructions to the employees about how they wanted their salads. They took their trays through different stations, and when they reached the last section, their salad bowl was taken. The lettuce and other veggies were chopped, and then the salad was tossed with the person's choice of dressing.

We kept walking and weaved through the concourse.

"Will we be able to find our way out?" I joked. "This place is huge."

"Look at that," Heather said. She pointed to an exit sign. "How convenient."

We took the stairs out of the concourse and ended up back near where the ice rink would have been if we'd been here during winter.

"And the tree is set up right here too," Heather said. "That's when it gets *really* crazy with tourists. Like, they should be banned-from-the-city crazy."

I grinned. "Good luck with that ever happening."

We passed a giant Nintendo store and I saw tons of kids and teens inside playing games on the giant TV screens and carrying around Nintendo memorabilia. *Jacob would love that,* I thought. I'd never be able to drag him out of the store.

"Did you see that restaurant we passed called Channel Four?" Heather asked.

"Yeah, it looked cool," I said.

"Everyone calls it C-Four," Heather said. "It's a place where lots of people who work in book publishing, TV, or other businesses in Rock Center come for lunch or dinner. They have the *best* chili ever there."

"Mmm," I said.

"It's almost time for Paul to pick us up," Heather said. "But I wanted you to see one more thing."

We walked a few more blocks and I saw lights that were bright even in the daylight.

"*That* is so awesome," I said.

Two vertical signs with the hall's name stretched up, and a horizontal banner was lit up with RADIO CITY MUSIC HALL. Just being in the city gave me a different energy.

In that moment, it started to hit me where I was. I was in New York City, standing in front of *the* Radio City Music Hall.

"Paul's over there," Heather said, tugging on my forearm. "We've got somewhere even cooler to go."

We walked to the car and I couldn't imagine anything more amazing than everything I'd just seen.

"Hi, Paul," Heather said when we got in the car. "We'd like to go to Dylan's, please."

"Wonderful," Paul said. "I think Sasha will enjoy that."

"I was going to take you to Times Square, but I figured that Paige had to have at least taken you, right?" Heather asked.

"Yeah, we did go there," I said.

"Good 'cause the place we're going is waaay better than insane Times Square," Heather said.

"What *is* Dylan's?" I asked. "I've never heard of it. Is it a clothing store or something?"

"Not even close," Heather said. "Just wait."

Paul pulled up to the curb, and Heather told him she'd text him when we were almost done.

We got out of the car and I looked around for a Dylan's sign.

"This way," Heather said. I followed her and we came up to a store with a front made entirely of glass. Colors radiated from inside and I looked at the black sign above the door. DYLAN'S CANDY BAR.

I looked at Heather. "Are you kidding me?"

Heather grinned, proud of herself. "They've got more than five thousand different kinds of candy."

"Oh. My. God. Why are we standing out here?!"

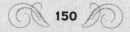

Laughing, Heather and I opened the door and stepped inside.

Charlie and the Chocolate Factory was one of my favorite books, and now it felt like I'd stepped into a page from the novel. I smelled so many kinds of chocolates, gummy bears, mints, and other scents that I couldn't distinguish one candy from the next.

The displays showing off oversize lollipops and giant chocolate bars were whimsical and colorful. The entire store was an explosion of color. Giant plastic jelly beans and candy bars hung above displays.

I saw dozens of plastic bins—each held one color of M&M's. Other bins held candies I'd never seen. I couldn't stop wandering. A wall was filled with Pez dispensers and every possible flavor of Pez.

I walked down an aisle that had displays of traditional candies—Snickers, Mr. Goodbar, Twix, and a zillion others—and it took all my strength not to grab a bag and fill it with candy.

"Come see this," Heather called, waving at me from a couple of aisles over.

I weaved through an aisle containing nothing but gummies and stood next to Heather. We both peered up at a glass case. Behind the case, black stars on white

paper made the glass box look even cooler.

In front of a tiny container of Skittles, a name tag said ASHLEE WRIGHT. The next box over had chocolate-covered cherries and the name of an Oscar-winning actor.

"These are all people who have stopped in the shop and told Dylan about their favorite candies," Heather said. "Pretty awesome."

"So cool," I said. "I love it!"

I kept reading the names, and it was fun to find out which celebs loved certain candies.

Heather pointed behind me. "They *do* have clothes here," she said. "They're in the most amazing colors and they have candy or candy sayings on them."

"I *have* to see that," I said.

Heather led the way to the apparel section. We went down clear stairs that looked as if they had candy trapped underneath them. I had to concentrate on watching where I was stepping instead of staring at the amazing steps.

Heather hadn't exaggerated about the colors of clothing. There were T-shirts, hoodies, tank tops, and pajamas in candy colors. I touched a cotton candy pink shirt that said I ♥ CANDY on the front.

"You should get that," Heather said. "It's cute."

She'd picked up a sky blue T-shirt with a conversation heart on it that said KISS ME.

"Only if you get that," I said. "I love it."

We kept looking through the clothing and accessories. There were necklaces, bracelets, and even rain boots—and everything was candy themed.

"We obviously can't leave without getting candy," Heather said.

"Obviously," I said. "I *so* need chocolate."

"And I'm really in the mood for something sour. Let's meet by the giant chocolate bunny in fifteen, cool?"

"Done."

Heather and I split up, and I grabbed a plastic bag like grocery stores use for fruit and veggies and picked up the scoop for peanut butter M&M's. I poured a half scoop into the bag and knotted it shut.

I picked up a couple of Snickers bars, a rainbow lollipop the size of my face, and a bag of gummy worms. I couldn't resist grabbing a few different kinds of Airheads. Then I checked the clock on my phone. Time to meet Heather.

We reached the enormous bunny at the same time. Heather had picked up a couple of boxes of Junior Mints, two bags of red licorice, and a few different candy bars.

"Ready?" she asked.

"So ready," I said. "I love it here, but I want to get out so I can start eating!"

Giggling, we headed for the checkout and awaited our inevitable sugar rushes.

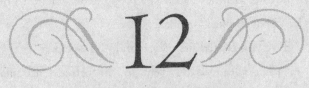

12

STOP SAYING SORRY

BACK IN THE CAR HEATHER LEANED FORWARD toward Paul. "I want to take Sasha to Dad's work."

I turned to Heather, half a gummy worm hanging out of my mouth, and looked at her as if she'd had a stroke or something. "You want to go to your Dad's office?"

Heather nodded. "Yeah. He'll be happy to show off his office, and you haven't been to Wall Street yet. The Financial District is at the tip of the island."

"How long will it take to get there?" I asked.

"I'm not psychic, Silver. It depends on traffic. But probably, like, twenty minutes," Heather said.

Twenty minutes to freak out about being in an office (read: small space!) with Mr. Fox. This seemed like a bad idea, but maybe Heather really thought it would help her relationship with her dad if she brought her friend to his office. That did kind of make sense.

"Have you visited his office lately?" I asked.

Heather shrugged. "I went to the office Christmas party, but that was the last time."

I tried to swallow, but my throat was dry. Mr. Fox was intimidating away from work—I couldn't imagine how he'd act at his job. He'd probably—no, definitely—be even more intense in business mode.

"This is the Financial District," Heather said once we were surrounded by imposing buildings. "Different from Midtown, huh?"

I looked out the car window and couldn't tilt my head enough to see the tops of the buildings. Each building was taller than the one next to it, and they all seemed to have a thousand gleaming windows. Men and women in suits and business clothes hurried up and down the sidewalks, carrying briefcases. I watched the women walking in high heels, wondering how they managed to walk so fast in heels like that on the NYC sidewalks. I'd fall on my face after one step.

"Here we are," Paul said. "I have to run an errand for your mom, Heather, then I'll be back waiting for you both, whenever you're finished."

"Thanks," Heather said.

We got out of the car and walked up to a revolving door. Heather walked through first, and I followed her. Inside the lobby, it was *freezing*. But it wasn't just the temperature that made the building feel subzero—it was also the lack of decor in the room. Everything looked so *cold*, and as if nothing was supposed to be touched. A glass table in front of a leather couch had business and financial magazines spread across it. There weren't any paintings on the white walls, and it didn't feel like a welcoming place.

Heather headed for a counter, where a burly security guard was eyeing us.

"Names?" he asked. He stared at us like we were kids who didn't belong in the building. A gold badge pinned to his white shirt said R. CURTIS. I tried not to shrink back behind Heather.

"Heather Fox and Sasha Silver," Heather answered. "We're here to see Mr. Fox, on the eleventh floor."

"Hold, please," the guard said. He flipped through a giant binder and ran his finger down a list of names. His big fingers punched the buttons on a phone.

"Hello, Eileen," he said. "I have Heather Fox and a friend to see Mr. Fox."

He listened, nodding. "Thank you. I'll send them up."

Mr. Curtis slid a clipboard toward us. "Sign your names here, and note the time."

Heather printed her name and wrote down the time. I did the same and handed back the clipboard.

Mr. Curtis got out from behind the desk and walked us up to an electric arm that blocked the elevators. He ran his plastic security pass over a blinking red light, and a beep sounded. The arm moved out of the way, and Mr. Curtis motioned for us to walk through.

"Thanks," Heather said. We walked toward the elevators, and Heather pushed one of the up buttons. The floor was white marble mixed with gold flecks, and it was a gorgeous space.

"Whoa," I whispered. "So high-tech."

Heather shook her head. "That guy must have been new. Usually they ask for a photo ID, scan it, and make you carry this printed-out sticker that you have to present if a guard asks for it."

"Seriously?"

"Yep."

"Scary." I couldn't imagine working in a building like this.

The elevator chimed and the doors opened. Heather and I stepped inside the red-carpeted elevator, and she pressed the button for the eleventh floor.

"I hope your dad isn't mad that we're here," I said.

Heather stared at me. "Did we not go over this, like, five minutes ago? He's all about ego—he's going to want to show off his office. Plus it'll probably get me on his good side for once, so just go with it."

"Okay," I said. I did want to help with her dad if I could.

I watched the numbers climb, and it felt like we'd just stepped into the elevator when it stopped at the eleventh floor. The doors slid open, and Heather and I walked down a short hallway to another lobby. This one was much smaller, and a woman sat behind a counter with a Bluetooth piece in her ear.

"Yes, Mr. Simon," she said. "I'm scheduling your four o'clock lunch right now." Her fingers were moving so fast over the keyboard in front of her—I had no idea how she did it and talked at the same time. Heather and I stopped in front of the desk and waited.

The woman pressed a button on her earpiece and looked up at us. "How may I help you?" she asked.

"We're here to see Mr. Fox," Heather said.

"Ah, right. Miss Fox," the receptionist said. "I called your father but got his voice mail. His schedule is clear at the moment, though, so feel free to wait in his office."

"Thanks," Heather said.

She turned away from the counter, and we walked down a gray-carpeted hallway. There was an office every few feet, and most of the doors were closed. I could hear people talking on their phones through the closed doors and the constant clicking of computer keys. Heather and I passed a small kitchen with a sink, espresso maker, and fridge.

"His office is right down here," Heather said as we sidestepped a woman taking a sip of a steaming cup of something as she hurried down the hallway.

We turned a corner and Heather paused for a second, then walked toward an open door.

"Dad?" she said, peering into the office.

I looked over her shoulder and saw that the office was empty. Behind Heather I stepped inside and looked at Mr. Fox's office. He had a giant, dark wooden desk with a leather chair. There was a slim computer monitor on the desk, and a giant mug of black coffee was next to the keyboard. A yellow legal pad had numbers scrawled on it, and a pile of papers were stacked in a neat pile at the end of the desk. A metal file cabinet was next to a black bookcase that was full of thick binders. Heather walked over and looked out the window.

"Nice office," I said. "It's, um, big."

But what I wanted to say was that the office was as impersonal as the lobby. There wasn't a plant, or anything that made it feel inviting. Then I realized what else was missing. There wasn't one family photo.

Not of Heather.

Or her mom.

Or the Fox family.

No posed pictures. No smiling photos from a family vacation. Nothing.

It had to hurt Heather's feelings to come to her dad's work and not to see one picture of herself anywhere. Both of my parents had family pictures in their offices at work. Dad even had one of me hugging Charm—he was part of the family too.

There were two chairs in front of the desk, and Heather sat down in one. I perched on the edge of the other chair, wringing my hands. I just wanted this to be over!

"Dad'll probably show us around the floor," Heather said. "I'm sure he'll want to introduce us—well, you, really—to some of his coworkers."

Fingers crossed they weren't as intense as Mr. Fox.

Footsteps approached the doorway, and Heather and I stood and turned to face the door.

"Please step into my office," Mr. Fox said. A man in a

suit and red tie stepped inside, briefcase in hand. I wondered if he was one of Mr. Fox's coworkers.

"Hi, Dad," Heather said with a smile when he walked through the door.

Mr. Fox's dark brown eyes narrowed when he saw us. "Heather?" he said. "What are you doing at my office during work hours?"

Heather's smile started to slip, but she managed to keep it on her face. "I wanted to show Sasha where you work," she said, her tone light. "She hasn't been to the Financial District before, and it's kind of cool that you work on Wall Street and everything."

Mr. Fox looked at the man, who stood off to the side. "I apologize, Henry. I'll be right with you."

"Heather," Mr. Fox said, taking her by the arm. "I'm with a client right now. You should have known better than to show up unannounced at my office. You and Sasha need to leave."

Heather swallowed, nodding. Her cheeks flushed, but she managed to keep her composure. "Sorry we interrupted."

Heather turned and I was right behind her on the way out of Mr. Fox's office.

I wanted to scream at Mr. Fox. He was without a doubt

the worst father on the planet. I understood that he had a meeting, but he could have asked us to wait a few minutes. And he didn't even introduce his *daughter* to his client. He'd treated Heather like a random kid who'd showed up in his space—not his daughter who'd been trying to make an effort with her dad.

"Heather," I said. I touched her elbow as we walked down the hallway. "Are you okay?"

Heather shrugged. "Whatever. Shocker. I should have expected it. Like he couldn't have taken five minutes to show us around. Or say sorry that we came down here to see where he works."

Her tone was angry, but there was a wobble to her voice. He'd gotten to her—not that she was going to admit that her feelings were hurt.

"Sorry."

"Stop saying sorry, okay?" Heather looked at me, and her eyes were slightly pink. "I'm not sorry. Just annoyed that I wasted my time. I *do* have more important things to do, you know, than come to Wall Street and sit around waiting for my dad. And I'm over talking about it."

I just nodded.

We got in the elevator, and this time it seemed to take forever to get back to the ground floor.

Heather flew out of the elevator the second the doors opened, and I almost had to jog to keep up with her. We walked past security, ignoring the sign-out sheet and the guard. Heather pushed the revolving door so hard, I had to wait for the second space to come around because the one behind her went by too fast.

Just like he said he would be, Paul was waiting in the car. He had the front windows rolled down and was doing a crossword puzzle. He looked up when he heard us approaching the car.

Heather yanked open the car door and actually slid across the backseat. I knew better than to make a joke about her earlier comment about how she didn't "slide."

Paul started the car and looked back at us. He saw Heather staring out the window, arms crossed.

"Was your dad out?" Paul asked, his tone gentle.

"Nope."

That was all Heather said.

Paul watched her in the mirror for a second and seemed to realize that something had happened.

"I'll take you home," he said.

The ride back from Wall Street to Park Avenue was silent.

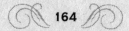

13

START THAT
HOMEWORK YET?

HEATHER HAD REGAINED HER COMPOSURE
by the time we walked through the door of her apartment. She looked as if nothing had happened a mere
half hour ago. But I knew she couldn't be over it so fast.
Heather had just put up the I-don't-care-and-I'm-fine
wall.

Without being asked, I followed her into her room. I
sat cross-legged on her bed and watched as she flicked on
the TV and flipped through channels.

"Exploring the city was really fun," I said, unsure how
she'd respond. "Thanks for showing me around."

Heather nodded, her eyes still on the screen. "Yeah.
Cool."

She stopped on one of my favorite channels, and it was

a rerun of *City Girls*—a show Paige and I had bonded over during my first day at Canterwood.

Heather sat in one of her chairs and drew up her legs as she watched the show. We watched the show for about fifteen minutes before I decided I had to distract her with something.

"I saw on the cover of *US Weekly* that Mira is dating Josh now," I said. Mira was one of the *City Girls*, who hadn't really had a boyfriend before.

Heather looked at me. "I saw that too. The article said she'd been crushing on him forever and she decided not to wait. She just went for it and asked him out."

"Hmm . . ." I said, smiling. "Sounds like she made the right choice—just going for it."

"Definitely," Heather said. "If she had a feeling that he liked her, why wait for him to ask her?"

"Does this sound like anyone we know . . . ?" I tilted my head suggestively.

Heather stared at me. "No . . . what are you talking about?"

I shrugged. "Oh, I don't know. There's this girl I know who has a crush on a guy. She thinks he likes her too, but he hasn't made a move yet. She talked to him at the Homecoming dance, but didn't pull a Mira."

Heather's mouth fell open in a clichéd teen-movie way. "Omigod! Are you kidding me?"

"No!" I said. "You should ask Troy out! Then you won't have to wonder if he likes you or not. You'll ask and he'll say yes or no, but I know he'll so say yes."

Heather shook her head, her blond hair flying. "No way! I'm not asking him out. I like him, but if he wants to go, he has to ask me. Otherwise, forget it."

My eyes landed on Heather's laptop. It was in sleep mode, the orange light blinking.

"You could e-mail him and say hi. See how break's going . . ." I said. "Or you could text him."

"And say what?" Heather unfolded her legs and sat up straighter. The glazed-over look was gone from her face. She was definitely distracted from the Father Fail that had occurred earlier.

"Just 'hi.' Ask him what he's doing. If he's bored at home, or if he's glad to be away from campus. Something casual."

Heather looked at her BlackBerry on her desk. She tucked her hair behind her ear, still looking at the phone.

"It'd be lame if I just texted him out of nowhere," Heather said. "I need a *reason*."

I paused, thinking. "Okay. Um . . . are you guys in any classes together?"

Heather smiled. "English."

"Did your teacher assign homework over the break?" I asked.

"Yeah, we have to read fifty pages of *The Outsiders* and write a five-page paper on it."

"Did you start yet?" I asked. "I haven't even looked at my homework."

"Please," Heather said. "Do you *think* I've done any homework yet?"

"That's your question. Tell him you haven't started yet and ask if he has. If he has, then you can ask him if the homework's hard or something. If he hasn't, then you guys can chat about *not* doing homework."

Heather nodded, thinking. "You know, I'm shocked right now, Silver."

"Why?"

"Because you had a good idea for once. I'm shocked. You *might* be smarter than you look."

"Thanks," I grumbled. "I think you've said that before. Are you going to text him or e-mail him?"

I jumped off the bed and walked over to Heather's laptop, my hand ready to open it.

"Fiiine!" Heather said. "I'll text him. It's not like I'm afraid to or anything. Whatever. It's just Troy."

I left her laptop and picked her up phone, handing it to her. Her fingers hovered over the keys for a while before she finally started typing. I sat across from her in the other chair, just waiting to see what she'd write. And I crossed my fingers that Troy would text her back.

"Here, this is what I'm sending?" Heather said. Her statement sounded more like a question. I looked at the screen that she held up to me.

Hey Troy—R u having a good break? Did u start English hmwk yet? I totally didn't—it's so lame. —H

"Perfect," I said. "That's supercasual and you're asking him questions instead of just saying hi and telling him all about your break. He's totally going to write you back."

Heather didn't look convinced. "You think?"

"Definitely. Send it."

Heather stared back at the phone, the send key option highlighted. "You do it."

She shoved the phone toward me. I stopped myself from laughing. Tough-girl Heather Fox, who acted as if she owned every inch of Canterwood, was insecure about something.

B-O-Y-S.

"No way," I said. "You wrote it. It's for Troy. *You* send it."

Heather held the phone in the air for a few more seconds before taking it back in front of her. She took a breath and pressed the button.

"There," she said. "Omigod, I can't take it back now. I texted Troy."

Heather tossed the BlackBerry onto her bed as if she couldn't stand holding it for another second.

We looked at each other, then burst into giggles.

"You texted Troy!" I said.

Heather kicked at my chair. "Shut up!" But she couldn't stop laughing. "He probably won't even—"

A chime from her bed cut her off. A red light started blinking on her phone and we both stared at each other.

"It's got to be, like, Julia or Alison," Heather said, shaking her head. "There's no way he'd write me back that fast."

"Go check it! It's so Troy." I motioned for her to get up and gestured toward the phone with a sweep of my arm.

Almost as if she was unsteady on her feet, Heather got out of her chair and picked up the phone off her bed. She pushed a couple of buttons and read. Her face gave away nothing.

"Well?!" I asked. "Say something! Who is it?"

Heather walked over, still with a poker face, and sat down. She held the phone up and grinned.

"It's Troy!" she said.

"Omigod! Told you!" I leaned forward and read his message.

Hey H! Having an awesome break. U? And no way did I start hmrk. It's BREAK. But when we start, if we get stuck or something, we could txt each other or IM. —Troy

Heather and I both started laughing again at the same time and she clutched her phone. I smiled secretly to myself, glad to have distracted Heather with something and curious to see what would happen with Troy.

14

ALL THE GLORY

IT WAS EARLY THE NEXT MORNING WHEN PAUL dropped us off at Chesterfield. Heather and I had come prepared for a long day of practicing. We'd talked over breakfast about the exercises we wanted to do, and how, since it *was* the middle of the week, we needed a day of serious practice.

Heather checked with Pam to make sure our horses were available, and they were. I was glad to ride Limitless again—he was a great horse, and this way I could focus on my riding instead of getting used to a new horse. Heather and I grabbed our tack and headed for Limitless's and Cora's stalls. Both horses had their heads hanging over the doors, and they looked at us as we approached.

"Hi, boy," I called to him. The bay's gentle brown

eyes watched me as I put down his tack and reached up to stroke his cheek. I closed my eyes for a second, pretending I was petting Charm. I missed him more every day, and I hoped he didn't think I'd abandoned him.

Charm knows better, I told myself, opening my eyes and looking at Limitless. I'd gone on break before and Charm had been superaffectionate when I'd gotten back, but he'd never acted as if he thought I'd deserted him.

Next to me Heather petted Cora and let herself inside the mare's stall. She led Cora out and tied the mare to her stall bars.

I unlatched Limitless's door and put on his lead line. Like Heather had done with Cora, I tied him up outside his stall. It seemed easier than trying to find a pair of free cross-ties. The stable was busy this morning. Horses and riders filled the aisle, hot walker, and wash stall.

"We should practice in one of the outdoor arenas," Heather said. "Inside's probably packed."

"Sounds good," I said. I grabbed Limitless's hoof pick out of his tack box and ran my hand down his right foreleg. "Hoof," I said, squeezing above his fetlock. He lifted his hoof from the ground and stood without leaning on me. Scraping the dirt and muck from his mostly clean hooves took only a few minutes. I skipped the rubber curry comb—his coat didn't need it—and picked up the dandy brush. As I ran it over his withers, I started thinking about last night. Heather and Troy had texted back and forth a few times after the first text. She'd told him about what we'd been doing over break and he'd told us about his break. He'd been having fun hanging out with his older brother and cruising around in his brother's new car.

I smiled, glad I could hide it behind Limitless. Heather had been so nervous about texting Troy—it had been shocking to see her that intimidated by a boy. But thinking about Heather's reaction to Troy made me think about how I'd first reacted when I started crushing on Jacob. His green eyes and light brown hair popped into my brain now, and I pictured his easy smile. I wondered what he was doing over break.

Stop thinking about Jacob! I wanted to smack myself in the face. I'd sworn off boys to focus on riding and school. No more boy drama. But I couldn't stop myself. I wondered if he was thinking about me. If he'd written me a text and deleted it because he'd thought I really didn't want to hear from him.

I pulled myself out of my thoughts when I realized I'd been standing next to Limitless's shoulder, not doing anything, while Heather was already starting to saddle Cora. I swept the body brush over Limitless and put his saddle pad on his back.

"C'mon, Grandma," Heather said. She took off Cora's halter and bridled her. "What were you doing over there? Sleeping?"

"You caught me," I said. "That's exactly what I was doing."

I put Limitless's saddle on and tightened the girth. He stood still while I untied him and put the reins over his head. He took the bit easily and I finished bridling him. Heather and I put on our helmets.

"Ready?" Heather asked, smoothing her red T-shirt.

"Let's go," I said.

We led the horses down the aisle, weaving through the traffic of horses and riders. I was glad when we got out of the congestion and stepped out of the stable. Today was the perfect day to ride outside—it was sunny without being blinding, warm without being hot enough to sweat, and there were only a few wispy clouds in the sky.

Heather and I stopped the horses to the side of the stable and mounted.

"Let's go to that arena," Heather said. She pointed to a large arena farther away from the stable than the others.

"Perfect," I said.

The horses' hooves were muffled by the grass as they walked at an easy pace toward the arena.

"I know we don't have time, but do you have a favorite trail here?" I asked.

Heather nodded. "Yeah—there's one I used to take whenever I needed a break. I love it because it's not one of those with a path worn into the ground because everyone takes it."

"I get that. I rode a school horse once that I'm sure could have taken himself on a trail ride—he knew every bend and turn on the path. Not very spontaneous."

"Exactly. So my trail was one that I made up when I took a wrong turn on a real trail. Then I just started taking that turn all the time. I showed it to my friends and we were the only ones who knew about it."

"What's the coolest thing on the trail?" I asked. Trail riding was one of my favorite things to do on horseback.

"It's this windy path with uncut grass that leads to an awesome lake," Heather said. "My friends and I used to— and this is soo lame—but we'd fill our bags with granola bars and water bottles and we'd wear our swimsuits under our riding clothes. We'd tie up the horses under the trees and swim in the summer and just have fun."

"That sounds like a great way to spend the summer," I said. "There weren't any lakes around my stable, but there was a creek. Charm and I splashed around it in during those days when it was so hot and gross during the summer."

Heather and I reached the arena, and I was excited to see there was already a jump course set up. It was complicated—with switchbacks, lots of verticals, and a bunch of oxers. If I'd been riding Charm, he would have dragged me toward the course.

"Want to warm up, then work on jumping?" I asked.

Heather nodded. "Definitely. That course looks exactly like what we need today."

We guided the horses toward the rail, staying out of the way of a man who was riding a sleek Standardbred. He was working the dark chestnut at a collected trot and it looked as if they'd been working for a while. The horse's mouth foamed at the bit and flecks had splattered his chest. The man rode as if he participated on the United States Equestrian Team. He wore a blue polo shirt, black helmet, and tall black boots. Just the way he sat on the horse made me realize he was at a level of riding I'd only dreamed about reaching one day. Dressage was my weakest area, and just watching him and the connection he had

with his horse made me want to try that much harder to improve.

I tore my gaze away from him so he wouldn't catch me staring, and focused my eyes between Limitless's ears. The bay moved into an easy trot when I asked him, and I sat to his trot for a couple of laps before starting to post. It took me only minutes to fall into the familiar rhythm of practice. Ahead of me Heather let Cora into a canter and she barely moved in the saddle as Cora cantered around the arena, her legs flashing as she moved.

I trotted Limitless for another half lap before I gave him rein and squeezed my legs against his sides. He eased into the faster gait and I had no trouble moving with him. He had one of the smoothest canters of any horse I'd ever ridden. I pulled him to a trot, crossed the arena, and switched diagonals. Heather followed us and we did this a couple of times before we pulled the horses up next to each other.

"You want to go first?" Heather asked. "I'll watch, and critique you when you're done."

"Sure. Thanks. Mind if I walk the course first?"

Heather shook her head. "Good idea. I'll do that now too. Save time."

We dismounted and led the horses toward the first

jump. I could have jumped it without walking it first, but it was a tricky course. I wanted to do the best job I could, especially since it was getting closer to the schooling show and I hadn't jumped Limitless before.

The man working on dressage pulled his horse to a halt, patted his neck, and started him at a walk in our direction.

"Omigod," I hissed to Heather. "Do you think he's going to say we were throwing off his practice or something?"

"I don't know!" she whispered back. "We stayed out of his way."

He stopped his horse in front of us and looked down with a smile.

"Hi," he said. "I'm Chad Warren. I couldn't help watching your warm-up. You're both quite talented. Keep it up."

He tipped his head at us and rode out of the arena.

Heather and I just stared at each other.

"Chad—"

"Warren," Heather finished.

"Omigod!" we both squealed at the same time.

"An Olympic contender just said we were talented! Omigod. Omigod," I said. "I had no idea it was him."

"Me either, obviously. Wow." Heather's cheeks were pink. "That was awesome."

"I can't believe we didn't recognize him," I said. "His face is only in every issue of *Young Rider* or *Horse Illustrated*."

"I know. But I'm kind of glad I didn't, actually. Then I might have gotten nervous and messed up."

"True," I said. "Just. Wow."

We led the horses forward and I counted strides in my head. I wasn't worried about forgetting the order of the jumps—that was straightforward. But I was a little concerned about the taller verticals and especially the faux flowers in a flower box on an oxer. I didn't know if Limitless was spooky about things like that. He didn't seem the type, but I wouldn't know for sure until I was out there.

Heather and I spent about ten more minutes checking out the jumps before we walked the horses back to the start.

"I think I'm ready," I said. I patted Limitless's neck and prepared to mount. I'd just stuck my toe in the stirrup iron when two tall shadows fell over us.

"Heather! And . . . Sarah. Hi," said Blake.

"It's *Sasha*," I said. I was tired of this girl acting like I wasn't important enough to remember my name. So. Rude.

"Hey," Emma added. "What're you guys doing on the ground? Did you fall?" Her gray gelding flared his nostrils as he tossed his head.

"Hardly," Heather said with a snort. "We were walking the jump course. We've got a schooling show coming up soon and—"

"We'll practice with you," Blake said, cutting off Heather. I glanced back and forth between them. *No one* ever interrupted Heather. That was, like, taught to every incoming student on the first day of school. The more I saw Blake, Emma, and Heather together, the less I was able to picture them all being close friends. I wondered if things had just fallen apart when Heather had left for Canterwood. Maybe Heather had been the leader of this clique and Blake felt threatened with Heather back in town.

"We were kind of going to coach each other," I said.

"Well, if you're practicing for a show," Emma said. "You should want as many people to critique you as possible." She smiled down at me from her bay gelding.

"Fine," Heather said.

What?! I didn't want to ride with these girls! Heather and I had staked out the jump course for ourselves— couldn't they go somewhere else?

"Sasha's riding first," Heather said.

"Perfect," Blake said.

My stomach churned. This reminded me of a lesson at Canterwood. Mr. Conner had made us all critique one another. Heather had torn up my ride and so had Julia and Alison. I had a feeling that was exactly what this was going to be.

But worse.

This was Blake's and Emma's territory. They treated Heather like a friend and an outsider at the same time. It had to be weird for her, too. But they'd all at least ridden together before. I'd never seen these girls ride. My gut told me that they were going to be pretty good if they were so quick to want to critique us.

I circled Limitless at a walk, then eased him into a trot. My fingers, already sweating, were making the reins slick. I let Limitless out of the circle and gave him rein, allowing him to move into a canter. He glided forward and I pointed him toward the first vertical. It was reasonably low with red-and-white poles.

Don'tmessupdon'tmessupdon'tmessup ran though my head at a dizzying pace. *Focus,* I told myself. I had to forget about Blake, Emma, and Heather and just concentrate on my ride. If I thought about them, I wouldn't be able to give my best.

Limitless was strides away from the vertical, his hooves pounding the dirt, so I started counting strides. *Four, three, two, one, now!* On *now*, I lifted slightly out of the saddle and moved my hands along his neck. Limitless jumped into the air, tucking his knees beneath him. He landed on the other side of the vertical and I almost cheered with relief when I didn't hear his back hooves click the rail. One down! Nine to go. . . .

Limitless cantered for six strides before we approached the first oxer. The spread was a couple of feet and didn't have any decorations on the sides to distract the horses. I let Limitless gain a fraction of speed so he had enough momentum to easily clear the spread.

At just the right moment, Limitless launched into the air, and for a short second we were airborne. There was no rush like it. Nothing made me feel *this* good. When I jumped I forgot about everything else going on around me. All I could hear was Limitless's breathing and his hooves hitting the ground. It was my job to get him around the course, and I couldn't have been more focused. Heather, Emma, and Blake had slipped away, and it was as if Limitless and I were the only ones in the arena.

Limitless reached the third jump—another vertical. This one was taller than the last and the rails were painted

with a dizzying yellow-and-black pattern. Limitless rocked back on his haunches and thrust himself into the air. I gave him enough rein to stretch his neck and he cleared the vertical without pause.

We moved toward the fourth jump, making a half circle and approaching another oxer. This one was made of dark rails that looked like logs. Greenery and flowers surrounded both sides. There was a lot for a horse to look at with this jump. Limitless flicked his ears back and forth, slowing a notch.

I squeezed my legs against his sides and drove him forward. If I let him slow, I risked him trying to run out or halt before the jump. I kept his canter steady and I didn't count strides this time—I kept all my focus on Limitless and making sure he jumped. His hoofbeats quickened as I encouraged him to canter faster, since this oxer had a wider spread. Limitless's pace increased, but I felt him start to pull to the right. He was *not* running out on the jump. Gently I pulled on the left rein and used my legs to press him back in line. We were strides away and I pushed him forward. He jumped, hesitating only slightly, and I felt him stretch over the spread.

We've got it, I thought. But I heard a thud as one of his back hooves clipped the rail. The rail tumbled to the

ground behind us and I fought back my disappointment. I didn't care as much that I'd messed up in front of Emma and Blake, but more that I hadn't been able to make a clean jump when I'd had plenty of time to correct Limitless.

But there wasn't time to dwell on it. We approached a double combination, and the timing on those is crucial. Limitless, recovered from his earlier scare, moved toward the first half of the combo with confidence. His long strides carried us to the jump and he cleared it with ease. Two strides later we were in the air again as he took the second half of the combo. We landed cleanly on the other side and it made me smile. That had been perfect.

The sixth jump, a faux stone wall, required us to make a sweeping turn around the corner of the arena, giving us plenty of time to face it. The extra time, though, caused problems for some horses. They couldn't see through a wall like they could other jumps, and it was another obstacle where run outs or refusals often happened.

But Limitless didn't seem fazed by the wall. His canter didn't slow as we moved toward the plastic stone. Just before the jump, I lifted out of the saddle and let him arch over the jump. He landed on the other side with a snort, proud of himself, and we headed for the final three jumps.

We cantered past Heather, Emma, and Blake, but

I didn't allow myself to look at them. I was *thisclose* to being done, and I wasn't going to get distracted now. The last three jumps were verticals, each increasing in height. Whoever had made this course had known how to challenge the horse when he was most tired, at the end of the course.

But Limitless wasn't showing any signs of fatigue. His stride hadn't slowed and he was moving with ease over each jump.

"We've got this, boy," I whispered to him. I knew Mr. Conner didn't like it when I talked to my horse during a ride, but I couldn't help it. Limitless was doing great.

We took the next blue-and-white vertical, hopped over the second, and four strides later, we'd approached the final jump. Limitless seemed to know this was the end of the course. He pushed off hard with his hind legs and snapped his forelegs under his body.

We'd nailed it.

I enjoyed the sensation of being in the air and grinned when we hit the ground. I didn't care about the rail we'd knocked—Limitless had made up for it in every other possible way. It wasn't his fault that he'd been scared, and I'd learned that I needed to work harder to calm my horse as soon as I realized he was uncomfortable with a jump.

 **186**

I let him canter in a half circle, then eased him to a trot. I wanted him to cool a bit before we stood on the sidelines and watched everyone else ride.

"Great job," I said, patting his warm neck. "You're such a good jumper."

He pointed an ear back at me, seeming to hear my praise.

We trotted around the arena once before we joined Emma, Blake, and Heather.

Heather was the first to smile. "Nice," she said.

Emma and Blake weren't smiling. They just sat on their horses' backs, staring at me.

"Thanks," I said. "Limitless is a really great horse."

"Yeah, he's a decent school horse," Blake said. "Let's talk about your ride." She turned to her friend. "Emma?"

Emma gave me a tiny smile. "You're definitely a great jumper. I think, though, you have a few issues with timing. I could tell you were counting strides, and I shouldn't have been able to. If you're going to count, at least make it invisible to us."

Heather and Blake nodded, and so did I. Emma was right about that. Sometimes it was obvious that I was counting strides instead of completely focusing on my horse and our ride.

"Heather?" Blake asked.

"It was a strong ride," Heather said. "You kept your focus and didn't let anything distract you." She gave me a tiny smile and I realized she was talking about Blake and Emma. "You've never jumped Limitless before, and it was a good round on a new horse."

I couldn't believe Heather was complimenting me—well, my ride—this much. We were friends now, but she still took any chance she could to correct mistakes in my riding.

"You do need to pay more attention to your hands on landings, though," Heather said. "Your hands moved around a lot when you landed, and you tugged on Limitless's mouth sometimes."

I cringed, feeling bad for Limitless. I hated watching other riders jerk on their horse's mouths and I felt bad I'd done it to him. Leaning down, I rubbed his shoulder.

"Sorry, boy," I murmured.

"Okay," Heather said, looking at Emma and Blake. "Who's next?"

"I'm ready," Blake said. She urged her horse forward, and I turned to Emma.

"What's her horse's name?" I asked.

"Walker," she said. "Her parents and trainer found him in Europe and had him shipped here."

Um, wow.

Blake's wavy black hair was loose under her helmet and it blew back behind her as she urged Walker into a trot. She took her time warming him up before letting him into a slow canter. She was nearly motionless on his back—just swaying gently with his gait. Her legs, clad in chocolate brown breeches, were light against Walker's side. She'd protected his legs with blue leg wraps, which drew more attention to his even stride.

I had a feeling there would be *very* little to critique about her ride.

Blake and Walker headed for the first jump, and I sat back in my saddle a little as the two cleared the vertical.

The girl was good.

Walker, whom I guessed to be a couple of years older than Charm, had definite experience. He seemed to know down to the split second when to take off for a jump. Every landing was soft, and Blake barely moved in the saddle when his hooves touched the ground after clearing a jump.

Blake was the opposite of what I'd expected. I'd thought she'd be forceful with her horse and willing to show off at any cost. Instead she was one of the quietest and calmest riders I'd watched in a long time.

When they reached the stone wall, I was mesmerized. Walker gathered himself, pushed off the ground, and glided over it. His gray coat was almost the same color as the plastic stone, and his form, and Blake's, were near perfect as they flew over the wall.

Blake and Walker finished their ride, and she slowed him to an easy canter, then a trot. She rode him up to us and there wasn't a hint of a smile on her face. I'd be grinning like an idiot after a ride like that.

"Go ahead," Blake said. She let go of Walker's reins and let them drop against his neck. "That ride was pathetic. I messed up so many times."

Whhooa! What?! I stared at Blake, waiting for her to say that she was kidding. There was no way she was serious. And even if she *had* messed up, I never expected her to be the type of girl who'd draw attention to her own mistakes. I'd definitely misjudged her—pegging her for one of those girls who thought every ride was perfect.

I looked at Emma, wondering if Blake's BFF would tell her the ride had been perfect and that Blake was crazy, or if she'd tell her friend what she really thought.

"Emma," Blake said. "What'd you think?"

"You're always way too hard on yourself," Emma said. "You know what you need to work on—sometimes you rely too much on Walker's experience and you go on auto-pilot. If you'd wanted to, you could have pushed him a little to remind him that *you're* in charge."

Blake nodded and I could tell she was really listening.

Blake looked at Heather. "You haven't seen me ride for a while. So what do you think?"

Heather pushed up her helmet. "I agree with Emma, honestly. You keep knocking yourself for rides that are great. It might help if you jump a less experienced horse a few times to remind yourself how it feels."

Blake picked up the reins again. "That's a good idea. I never would have thought of that."

The three girls looked at me since it was my turn to critique Blake. I had to say *something* or she'd think I was sucking up. But everything had already been said—I really hadn't seen other mistakes in her ride.

"I think Emma and Heather covered it all," I said. "You've got a great horse who's willing to do anything you ask, and you two definitely make a great team. I enjoyed watching you ride."

"Thanks," Blake said. She patted Walker's neck and eased him next to Emma's horse.

"Go ahead, Heather," Emma said. "I'll go last."

"Okay," Heather said. Her face was tight as she trotted

Cora forward. She had to be feeling pressure to ride well. Riding in front of her old friends, who were now her competition, couldn't be easy. I took a deep breath, glad my own ride was over. I crossed my fingers that Heather would ride as well now as she did at school.

Heather and Cora took the first vertical—leaping it gracefully—and I knew then that Heather didn't need *any* luck for this ride.

She urged her horse forward, looking confident and as if she were the only one in the arena. Cora responded well to her, and it seemed to take them only a matter of seconds before they'd cleared all ten jumps. I'd noticed only a couple of minor mistakes, and it was a ride Mr. Conner would have been proud of.

Heather lined Cora up in front of us and patted the mare's neck.

"Well, you've certainly improved since you got to Canterwood," Blake said. I bristled a little at the back-handed compliment. "You're still making some of your old mistakes. Guess the YENT hasn't trained them out of you yet."

Heather's cheeks went pink. But she quickly regained her composure and tossed back her head. "And what mistakes would those be?"

"You didn't keep enough forward motion," Blake said. "Cora's canter wasn't steady throughout the course, and for a second I thought she was going to break into a trot."

"She wasn't even close to trotting," Heather argued. "Yeah, her canter did slow *once* when I wanted her pace steady, but she was far away from trotting."

Blake smirked, shaking her head. "Heather, Heather. I thought the whole point of this was to be honest and critique each other. I listened to you, Emma, and Sasha."

Wow, that was, like, the first time she got my name right.

"Because what we told you was actually true," Heather said. "If you'd pointed out something that had really happened, I would have listened and tried to use it the next time I jumped."

"Heather would have listened if you'd given her good feedback," I added.

Heather and Blake glared at each other. Uh-oh. . . .

"Do you have anything to add that really happened, or not?" Heather asked. "'Cause if you do, I'm listening."

Blake stared at her. "You know what, *this* is why we don't talk anymore. Ever. You went off to Canterwood thinking it's a better school, which it's not, and just

193

because you made the YENT, you think you're the best rider who ever got on a horse."

Heather's face reddened and she set her jaw.

"Well, guess what?" Blake continued. "You're. Not."

I sat unmoving in Limitless's saddle. This was about to get U-G-L-Y.

"I never said I was the best rider," Heather said. "And FYI, the YENT has nothing to do with this. You gave me criticism that wasn't true. Like I already said, if you'd told me something I could improve on, I would have taken it. But you're just making things up to make yourself look like a better rider. And *don't* trash talk my school."

"Guys," Emma interjected, "let's not—"

"No, Emma," Blake said, holding up a gloved hand. "We're having this conversation. Heather, you left our old school because you thought we weren't good enough for you. Fiiine. Like any of us cared. Truth? We were kind of glad when you left."

"Excuse me?" Heather said. Her tone was rising with every word. "You were *glad*? We were *friends* when I left!"

My eyes met Emma's and we shared a look of mutual discomfort. How had things gone so wrong so fast?

"No, you tried to lead Emma and me around like puppies while you got all the glory for being the star

rider," Blake snapped. "Well, you're gone now. You're not the best at Chesterfield anymore."

Heather laughed dryly. "You think I came back over break to stage a takeover and reclaim whatever 'star' status you seem to think I had?"

Blake shook her head. "No. Because you think we're all beneath you, anyway, since you made the YENT. But like I care—now that you're gone, Emma and I are getting all the attention and work we need to make the YENT during the next tryouts. And *you* won't be there to distract us."

"Wow," I said. "Who are you going to blame if you don't make the YENT? Sad for you that Heather won't be here."

Heather straightened slightly—she was probably as surprised as I was that I'd just stood up for her.

"Sasha and I are done in the arena," Heather said. "Enjoy. I wouldn't want to stay and be a 'distraction.'"

She pulled Cora out of line and started her at a trot out of the arena. I kept my gaze off Emma and Blake and let Limitless follow Cora. Heather and I drew the horses even with each other, and I looked over at her.

"Sorry," I said. "Blake was a total jerk. I can't believe she said all of those things."

"Who cares about Blake?" Heather said. "Some friend she was. They can think whatever they want about me. I really don't care."

We were silent for a few seconds as we slow the horses to a walk.

"Where should we practice now?" I asked. "Is there someplace else we can go, where they won't be watching us?"

Heather paused, thinking. "You know what? I think that was enough of a practice. This is *break*. Want to trail ride?"

"Sounds perfect," I said. "As long as you're sure you don't want to work on flatwork or anything."

"Nope," Heather said. "We'll still practice this week, but you know we'll be riding all the time once we get back to Canterwood to prep for the schooling show. We deserve a little time off."

"Agreed."

This was *so* unlike Heather. Usually she was the one insisting we practice until we dropped. But maybe she was finally realizing that we didn't have to ride until we were exhausted to be prepared. We worked as hard as we could, but I still wanted to have *fun* riding. And a trail ride in a new area sounded amazing. I only wished Charm were

here since I knew how much he'd enjoy exploring the new trails.

"C'mon," Heather said. "I'm going to show you the coolest trail."

And, tossing quick smiles at each other, we let our horses walk side by side away from the stable, Blake, Emma, and all of their drama.

Soon Chesterfield was well behind us, and Heather and I were relaxed in our saddles as we headed for a line of trees.

"I love riding in the woods," I said. "It feels so far away from everything."

"Me too," Heather said. "I need to take more time to trail ride at Canterwood. You've probably found trails I haven't."

"Probably," I said, smiling. "I used to trail ride a lot with Callie . . .."

For a second I wished I hadn't brought Callie up. Just like I wanted to stop thinking about Paige. And just like I wanted to stop thinking about Jacob.

Heather didn't press me on the Callie comment. We entered the woods and let the horses amble at their own pace down a grassy path. A line of grass had been trodden by horses walking over the same area again and again.

We started up a gentle hill and I leaned forward in the saddle, giving Limitless extra rein. He stretched his neck and took the climb with ease. Cora snorted and stepped sideways around a scary-looking clump of grass. Heather pressed her boot against Cora's side, straightening her before she could bump into Limitless. The mare listened and eased sideways.

The hill leveled, and Heather turned Cora between two oak trees.

"Everyone else usually keeps going that way," she said. "But I think this way is so much cooler."

A year ago, if Heather had asked me to trust her and follow her down a hidden trail, I would have refused, thinking she'd try to ditch me and get me lost in the woods. Now things had changed so much between us. She'd been a better friend than I'd expected, and we'd had a lot of fun together over break. I was actually kind of sad that break was almost over.

We reached a wide but shallow creek, and I pressed my boots against Limitless's sides to keep him moving forward. But he had no issues with the creek. He walked right through the clear water and his shoes clinked against the pebbles and rocks that lined the creek bed. Beside us, Cora walked through the water as easily as Limitless did.

The horses maneuvered up the creek bed and reached a flat meadow.

"If you want, we can gallop them to the other side of the field. It's safe," Heather said.

"Definitely," I said. I couldn't wait to try riding Limitless at a gallop.

"Then let's go!" Heather urged Cora into a trot, and then a canter.

I gave Limitless rein and we charged after them. We pulled even with Heather and Cora, and Heather and I traded looks. At the same second, we let the horses into gallops. Limitless stretched his neck, and I bent lower over his withers, encouraging him to move as fast as he wanted.

His long legs carried us easily over the ground, and wind rushed in my ears and blew back my ponytail. Adrenaline kicked in and I hoped the field would stretch forever; I never wanted Limitless to stop galloping. It was such a rush!

Beside us Cora kept up—not letting Limitless get an inch in front of her. But this wasn't a race. Heather and I really were galloping our horses for fun, and no one was trying to outdo the other. It felt good to just *ride*. No competition. Just riding, and loving every second of it.

A line of trees appeared in the distance, and I eased

back on the reins. Limitless responded, slowing to a fast canter. Heather and I let Cora and Limitless canter for several more yards before we slowed them to a trot, then a walk, just before reaching the trees.

"That was amazing," I said. "I'd forgotten how much I love galloping."

"I know," Heather said. "That's the perfect place to do it."

We smiled at each other and I let out a happy sigh. This break was not like I'd anticipated it to be. It was way better.

15

CALL A HOTLINE

LATER THAT NIGHT I WANDERED DOWN THE
hall toward Heather's room. We'd finished dinner, and
Heather had invited me to come to her room to watch
movies and talk about what we were going to do tomorrow.

Heather was sitting cross-legged on her bed in flare-
legged gray sweat pants and a baby-doll T-shirt. She was
typing on her laptop, looking focused.

"Ooh," I said, folding my arms and grinning. "Are you
e-mailing a certain guy?"

Heather looked up as if I'd startled her. "What?"

I headed for a chair. "Hmm . . . I wonder. Troy! Are you
e-mailing him?"

Heather closed her laptop lid. "No, I was IMing Julia."

"Oh. How's her break going?"

Heather got up and put her laptop on her desk. "Fine. She's having fun. So let's see what's on TV before we start a movie."

"Sure."

I relaxed in the chair, putting my feet up on the ottoman. My dorm room was going to feel so small compared to this.

Heather turned on the TV and flipped through the channels. The Food Network for Kids popped up, and Paige's green eyes and red hair filled the screen.

"And now," Paige said, "I'm going to teach everyone how to make ten-minute quesadillas. They're fast, fun, and supereasy to make."

I wanted to look away, but I couldn't. Just hearing Paige's voice, even through the TV screen, made me sad and angry at the same time.

"Nothing good on TV," Heather said, switching on the DVD player. She glanced at me. "Has Paige texted you or anything since your fight?"

"A bunch of times," I said. "She keeps saying that she wants to apologize. I don't know—I mean, she's my best friend and I miss her. But I'm not ready to hear her apology yet. I know she's sorry, but I need time first."

"There's nothing wrong with that," Heather said.

"What she said to you at the dance was awful. And this probably sounds harsh, but she needs to take some time too and come up with a really good apology."

"I agree," I said. "I don't want her to apologize if she doesn't completely understand why I was so upset. I *know* she didn't mean what she said, but she still said it. The fact that she would just makes me wonder if we're not as close as I thought we were. And I really, really hope that's not true."

"I think your friendship with Paige will be fine," Heather said. "When you're ready, you'll listen to her apology, and then you can decide for yourself if whatever she says is enough."

I nodded.

"Thanks for talking to me about it," I said. "I'd probably go crazy if I didn't have anyone to talk to."

"We're not making this, like, a regular thing," Heather said, looking at me sideways. "Call a hotline if you need to vent." And the old Heather was back.

16

JUST PRETEND YOU DON'T KNOW ME

I'D WOKEN UP EARLY, EXCITED ABOUT THE day. Heather hadn't told me anything, of course, about what we were doing today. She liked playing tour guide more than she let on, and she was proud of her city. I slid my feet into my platform sandals and glanced at my outfit in the mirror. Black skinny jeans with one of my new shirts—the scoop-neck seashell-colored one. I grabbed my purse off the bed and walked to the foyer. At least we didn't have to worry about a run-in with one of her parents this morning. Mr. Fox had left for work hours ago, and Mrs. Fox had gone a while ago to a spin class.

Heather was waiting, arms across her chest. "When I said we were going at ten, I didn't say it just because."

I turned and looked at one of the wall clocks. "It's not even ten-oh-two," I said. "Barely."

Heather pulled open the door, muttering something under her breath.

We got in the car and Paul greeted us with a smile. I was going to miss him when we went back to school. I'd gotten used to seeing him every day, even though I hadn't been here all that long.

"Where to this morning, ladies?" he asked.

"Central Park, please," Heather said.

I turned, grinning. "Central Park. Omigod, I can't wait! I went there with Paige, and we ended up having to leave early. I was so sad that there wasn't more time to explore."

"Jeez, calm down," Heather said. "You're going to be tired before we even start walking around. Did you see any of the Great Lawn?"

"I don't think so," I said. "What's there?"

Heather checked her phone. "Like, a zillion things. Since we're taking drama, I thought it would be cool to go because there's tons of theater and Shakespeare stuff in that area."

"I've read about that," I said. "It's supposed to be amazing." I knew I sounded like one of those dorks

who read an NYC guide book from cover to cover, but I couldn't help it.

As Paul drove down the crowded streets, I stopped myself from pressing my nose against the window like a kid. It didn't take too long to reach the park, and Heather told Paul she'd text him when we were ready.

We got out of the car on Fifth Avenue and started toward the park. We walked down the sidewalk and I stared at a gorgeous sculpture.

"*Alice in Wonderland* characters," I said. "Wow. I love that book."

Alice sat on top of a huge mushroom, with the Mad Hatter and the March Hare nearby. I loved the Cheshire Cat over her shoulder. We kept walking, and it was as if I had lost track of time. There was so much to see, and with every step we wound our way deeper into the park. Heather and I walked up to a grassy hill, passing a beautiful stone archway. On the hill, people were sprawled out on the grass. Some were on blankets having a late breakfast, others were walking dogs, and some were reading.

I loved the busyness of NYC, but it felt good to get away from the noise, crowds, and concrete. It was hard to comprehend that a giant park, with so much grass and so many trees, was in a place as metropolitan as NYC.

We kept walking, not in any particular direction. We just walked, and I took in the quietness around us.

"Omigod!" I yelped. I jumped sideways and crashed into Heather.

"What?! Omigod! Sasha!" Heather grabbed my upper arm and righted herself before she fell over.

My heart pounded as if I'd just run through the entire park. "I'm so sorry," I said. "But *that* scared me!" I pointed up.

Crouched on a rock was a statue of a panther. It looked ready to pounce, and the life-size cat had caught me by surprise. It looked so real. I wondered if the artist had spent time watching and studying panthers before making the sculpture.

"You've *got* to be kidding me!" Heather said, glaring at me. "You were just scared by a *statue*. That's ridic even for you, Silver." She glanced around. "I really hope no one saw that."

I held back a giggle. Now that my heartbeat was returning to normal, the whole thing was actually kind of funny.

"If anyone asks you why your friend freaked out, you can totally say you don't know me at all," I said. "There."

Heather rolled her eyes and we started walking again. A few minutes later I stopped midstep.

"Is that . . ." I started, but couldn't finish my sentence.

"Yep," Heather finished. "It's a mini-castle. In Central Park."

"Whoa," I whispered.

Heather, amused by my staring, smirked. "It's called Belvedere Castle. They do tours and stuff, but we don't have time today."

"It's gorgeous," I said. I'd never seen anything like it in real life. The Gothic-style castle made me feel transported to another time. I half-expected women in ball gowns and jewels to step out of the castle and wait for carriages to whisk them off to a fancy dance.

"It is beautiful," Heather said, twisting her hair into a low ponytail. "Whenever I've walked by it, I've always envisioned a stable behind it and girls our age riding their horses sidesaddle."

I could see what she was talking about. "They'd have cute stable boys rushing to their every need."

Heather laughed. "That sounds like a line from a romance novel."

We grinned at each other and kept walking. The September sun was directly overhead now, and I enjoyed the gentle breeze that blew through the park. With every step we took deeper into the park, the more birds and squirrels I noticed. And the squirrels didn't seem to be afraid of anything or anyone. They perched on benches and took their time crossing in front of people on the sidewalk. And for the next few hours Heather and I wandered around the park, seeing where we'd end up.

"I'm starving," Heather said much later. "You ready to go?"

"Agreed. Lunch sounds awesome."

Heather texted Paul, and I couldn't wait to see where we were going next. Heather hadn't picked one thing all week that hadn't been awesome.

"After lunch we'll go back to my place, and then tonight I know exactly where I want to go for dinner," Heather said.

"Are you going to tell me where we're going?" I asked.

"Hmm . . ." Heather shrugged. "Why not? We're going to a place I know you've heard of."

"Really? Where?"

Heather grinned. "Oh, just a little place called Butter."

"No. Way. Nooo, seriously?! *Butter?*" I tried not to freak out in Central Park. Butter was the hottest restaurant that morphed into a celeb-packed club at night. It was only mentioned at least two or three times in every issue of gossip mags.

"We could go somewhere else if that sounds, like, boring to you," Heather teased.

We both started laughing and were still giggling a couple of minutes later when Paul pulled up.

17

DON'T MAKE ME HEIMLICH YOU

WE HAD TO LEAVE SOON FOR BUTTER—
I never wanted to stop saying the restaurant's name—
and I was a mess. I couldn't decide what to wear, my
freshly washed hair was half up and half down as I straightened it, and I'd redone my eyeliner three times. My shaky
hands had kept drawing squiggly lines.

"Okay," I said aloud to myself. "Stop and do one thing
at a time. It's just a restaurant and you're going to be
totally fine."

"I didn't know a crazy person who talked to herself
was staying with me," Heather said, poking her head into
my room.

"I can't decide what to wear and we're leaving soon!"
I said. "You're ready to go and I'm not even close."

Heather was dressed just right for dinner in a deep red halter dress and black wedges. Her hair was loose around her shoulders and she'd given it soft waves with a curling iron.

Heather eyed the mass of clothes thrown on my bed. "Calm down, Silver. We're just going out to eat. Do your hair so you don't look like a weird poodle, and I'll be back in a sec—I've got a dress you can borrow." She waved her hand dismissively at my pile of clothes. "I don't have to look through any of that to know you don't have something for Butter."

She disappeared and I picked the flatiron up off the dresser and stared in the full-length mirror as I went back to smoothing my hair. Heather reappeared a few minutes later, just as I was unplugging the flatiron.

She held out a dress to me. "What do you think?"

It was a strapless black cocktail dress. Simple, but sophisticated at the same time. In this dress, I'd actually look as if I fit in at Butter.

"Ooh," I said. "It's perfect! I can really borrow it?"

"I have a zillion of them," Heather said. "I won't even care if you spill something on it."

I took the dress, making a face at her. "Thanks for the vote of confidence."

Heather walked back to the doorway. "Your hair is done and you have a dress. Finish your makeup and meet me in my room when you're done. And make it fast."

I nodded and grabbed my makeup bag and Heather's dress. I sprinted for the bathroom and got dressed, loving how the cocktail dress made me feel pretty and confident. Taking a breath, I started over on my eyeliner, and this time I managed to draw straight black lines. I dusted shine-absorbing powder over my T-zone and added peachy blush to my cheeks. Tonight I wanted the focus to be on my eyes, so I used clear gloss on my lips.

There. Done.

I left the bathroom and slipped my feet into my black kitten heels. Anxiety over getting ready melted into excitement. We were going to Butter!

I hurried down the hallway to Heather's room. She was on her laptop, sitting in one of her chairs.

"I'm ready," I said.

"Obviously," Heather said. "One sec. Let me tell Alison we're going and log off IM."

"Okay."

I rummaged through my purse and pulled out my phone. I hadn't checked my e-mail in forever. I tried to log in and got an error message.

Huh.

I tried again, and when I got another error message, I clicked it so I could figure out what was going on.

You're already currently logged in on another computer. Please log off and try again. If you think you've reached this message in error, contact Customer Support.

It was definitely a mistake—I wasn't on my e-mail anywhere else. Ugh—I'd try again later. I closed my phone as Heather shut her laptop lid. She grabbed her purse off her bed, and we walked to the front door.

The Fox penthouse was silent.

"Should we tell your mom we're leaving?" I asked.

"Nope. I told her what time we were going and where. And do you see her running out here to say good-bye?" Heather asked, her voice low.

I didn't answer the question I knew was rhetorical.

We left the apartment and took the elevator to the ground floor. Outside the sun was setting, and lights were starting to illuminate the city. We got in the car and I smoothed Heather's dress as Paul drove us forward.

"Have you been to Butter before?" I asked Heather.

"A few times," she said. "Depending on the night, it can get pretty crowded. But I didn't have any trouble making reservations for tonight."

That made me relax a little. I was glad my first trip to a superstar restaurant wouldn't be packed.

"Does it really look just like it does in magazines?" I asked.

Heather glanced at me, and passing car lights reflected in her eyes. "Yes, Silver. It does."

I could tell she wasn't really annoyed—just amused at my babbling. Paul pulled up to the curb and Heather opened the door.

"See you in a couple of hours," she said to him.

"Have a great dinner, girls," Paul said.

I got out of the car after Heather and stared at the restaurant's glass window. The word BUTTER looked back at me, and I couldn't believe where I was standing. My fave celebs had walked *right here*. It was crazy to think about!

"We have to, you know, go inside to eat," Heather said.

"Right. Inside."

And when we stepped inside, everything Heather had said about Butter was true. It looked exactly like the magazine photos. Omigod. The decor was elegant but modern. The ceiling was curved, and there were potted trees in almost every corner of the room and along the walls. The soft lighting gave the place a, well, buttery glow.

"We have reservations under Fox," Heather told a man

in a suit and tie. He typed something in in his laptop, then smiled at us.

"Of course," he said. He picked up two menus. "Right this way, please."

Heather and I followed him downstairs to a dining area, which looked *nothing* like the restaurant's entrance. The low ceiling had flattened out and was covered with tree vines. Candles were on every table, and their light flickered across the tables. It was casual, but one of the coolest places I'd ever seen.

The waiter walked us over to a corner table. "Is a table in the Birch Room suitable?" he asked.

"Perfect," Heather said.

Our table was in front of a half-circle green couch. Heather and I slid onto the couch and the waiter filled our water glasses. He placed a basket of breadsticks in front of us with a small bowl of olive oil.

"May I get you anything to drink?" he asked.

"I'll take a bottle of Perrier," Heather said. I'd never had that kind of fancy water, but I'd seen it in the Trio's suite.

"One bottle of Perrier," the waiter said. He looked to me. "And for you?"

"The same," I said. "Perrier sounds great."

"I'll be right back," the waiter said.

He walked away and I glanced around. I loved the curved couches and how the entire room was filled with candles. I glanced up at the vines on the ceiling.

Heather caught my gaze and looked up too. "It's so creative," she said. "I'd never be able to come up with anything like that. It could have turned out creepy or something, but the birch wood looks so sophisticated."

"It does," I said. "It must have taken forever to design this room."

"Let's check out the menus so we're ready to order when the waiter gets back," Heather said.

"Good idea." I picked up my menu from the thick white tablecloth and opened it. "Wow. Everything sounds so good!"

I decided against "seared Hudson Valley foie gras" since I didn't know what that was and was afraid to ask. But there were so many other choices that sounded so good.

Heather nodded. "I know. Their food is awesome."

The waiter appeared with our drinks and set the pretty green glass bottles in front of us. He held up his pad of paper. "Are you ready to order, or do you need more time?"

Heather looked at me and I nodded. "We're ready," she said.

"Go ahead," I said.

Heather looked at the menu. "I'll have your seared local mackerel and a romaine salad."

"All right," the waiter said. "And for you, miss?"

"I'll take the grilled chicken and the soup of the day," I said.

"Fantastic," the waiter said. "We have a delicious lobster bisque that I'm sure you'll enjoy." The waiter closed his notepad and dipped his head at us. "I'll be back as soon as possible with your orders."

"Thank you," Heather and I said.

I glanced around, trying not to look as if I was scanning the place for celebs, even though I *so* totally was.

"Even if Scott Ryder would happen to walk by," Heather said, "he'd be so scared of you and your Oh-my-God-I'm-totally-gonna-freak face. Chill."

"Right, sorry," I said. I picked up a breadstick and dipped it in the olive oil.

"And *no* double dipping," Heather said. "Eww."

"You'd definitely catch something from me *now*, especially since, I don't know, I've been using your lip gloss and we've been living together for almost a week."

Heather rolled her eyes at me and tore off a piece of breadstick. The waiter served our soup and salad, and we downed them.

People on the outside probably thought we *hated* each other and couldn't begin to understand why we were hanging out together or even friends. But the way Heather teased me wasn't the same anymore. She wasn't attacking me with personal digs that would have made me furious or on the verge of tears. We were bantering back and forth, and it was meant to be playful—not to hurt anyone.

I was surprised to look up a few minutes later and see our waiter—they served food fast at an upscale place like this.

The waiter set down our plates and collected our soup and salad bowls.

"I'll be back to check on you in a few minutes," he said.

"Thanks," Heather and I said.

Heather took a bite of fish, and I started on my chicken. It. Was. So. Good. I'd never thought herb-roasted chicken could taste this good. I kept taking bigger bites, then glanced at Heather as I felt her eyes burning into me.

"I'm not doing the Heimlich on you if you choke because you're shoveling food into your face," Heather said.

Yeeeah, okay. She was kind of right. I slowed down and enjoyed my food. The lobster bisque had been amazing, just like the waiter had promised, and I loved the Perrier water. I think it ruined my taste for any other kind of sparkling water.

I raised my fork to my mouth and turned to Heather. "This place is really awesome—"

I stopped midsentence when I saw Heather's eyes widen. She turned to me.

"Um," she said. "Uh."

I'd never heard her talk like that.

"What? What's wrong?" I looked up and almost dropped my fork.

18

SHOT DOWN

PAIGE AND TWO OF HER FRIENDS WERE WALKING toward us. They were following a waiter, who set menus down on a table just a few feet away from Heather and me.

Paige hadn't seen us yet. I didn't know what to do! She was going to spot us eventually, and then what? If she wanted to talk to me alone, I wasn't sure I was ready for that. Even though I knew I couldn't keep avoiding the situation forever, I still didn't feel ready to talk about it. Especially not when I was having such a fun dinner.

I kept my eyes off Paige's table and concentrated on my food. Every few seconds I felt Heather's eyes on me. I wanted to ask her what I should do, but it wasn't her fight. She'd already given me enough advice. And there wasn't anything to do. If Paige *had* seen me, she wasn't approaching me. So maybe she'd gotten the hint from my nonresponses to her texts that I wasn't in a place where I wanted to talk and I'd come to her when I was.

"She has to know better than to come over here," Heather said, her tone low. "She's with her group of friends and you're with me. It would be so uncool if she came over."

Heather had just finished her sentence when movement across the room got my attention.

Paige, standing, whispered something to her friends and started walking in our direction. She, too, was dressed for Butter in a silver and black bandage dress. I couldn't help looking at her face, and our eyes were locked as she walked over to my table.

"Sasha," Paige said, her voice soft. "Hey, Heather."

Heather opened her mouth, probably about to say something snarky, but I didn't need her to get involved.

"Paige," I said. "Heather and I are in the middle of dinner. I know you want to talk about what happened, and we will, but now's not a good time."

I saw the hurt on Paige's face and it made me feel awful, but she'd been horrible to me the night of the party. I wasn't ready to talk yet.

"Sasha." Paige's green eyes stayed on mine. "Please.

Can we just step outside for two seconds? We can definitely talk more at school, but please, just let me talk to you for a minute."

I paused. Part of me wanted to say yes. But a bigger part said no.

"Sorry," I said. "I hope you have fun with your friends. But Heather and I are finishing our food, and then we're going back to her place. We'll talk at school."

"Bye," Heather said to Paige in a cheery tone.

I didn't want Heather being mean to Paige, so for Paige's sake, I hoped she just walked away.

And with a defeated look, that's exactly what she did.

19

PHONE FEAR

HEATHER AND I FINISHED OUR DINNER AT Butter and left. I couldn't wait to get out of there and back to Heather's. We didn't talk about Paige for the entire car ride. Heather seemed to sense I didn't want to talk about Paige—and she was right.

We got back to her penthouse, changed, and met up in her room.

"Want to have popcorn or something and watch reruns of something dumb but entertaining?" Heather asked.

"Def," I said.

I noticed Heather staring at her phone.

"What's up?" I asked.

"Nothing," Heather said. She paused. "Well, I don't

know. Troy and I have been texting a lot and I was thinking about calling him."

"You should!" I said. "Just be supercasual and say hi and ask what he's doing."

"Isn't calling him like, weird, though? Would he think that was strange if I just called him instead of texting like we've been doing?"

I shook my head. "No way. I think he'd be surprised and happy that you called. Just do it."

Heather got up from her chair and walked over to her phone. She put her hand on it, then yanked it back as if the phone were was hot.

"Nah, never mind. I'll just text him later."

Heather's cheeks turned the same color as her bright pink T-shirt.

"C'mon. Heather Fox doesn't get scared of anything. Call him. He might not even answer—you never know."

That seemed to make Heather relax a little. "That's true. Hopefully I'll just leave a message and that'll be it."

"Right. And if he answers, you're not going to be on the phone forever. Just chat a little and tell him you have to go do something. Then there won't be awkwardness or anything."

Heather took a deep breath. "Good idea. Okay. Whatever. I'm calling him."

She grabbed the phone and scrolled through her address book for his number. I hid a smile. I understood how she felt about being nervous, but it was also amusing to see her this intimidated by a *boy*. The girl would jump stone walls, gallop her horse at top speed across a pasture, and deal with her crazy dad. But a boy? Terrified.

Heather sat beside me on her bed and held the phone between us so we could both hear. It rang once and then she pulled the phone away from her ear and ended the call.

"What are you doing?!" I asked. "You just hung up!"

"I know!" Heather flopped onto her back and covered her face with a pillow. "Omigod. I just called him and hung up. That was superlame."

"Uh, yeah, but I think you have a little more to think about than it being 'lame.'"

"What're you talking about?" Heather uncovered half her face.

I held up her phone. "There's this magic thing called caller ID. He's going to see you called him since you're already in his address book."

The pillow went back over Heather's face. *"Omigod!"* Her scream was muffled.

I reached over and touched her shoulder. "He might think you called him by accident. I dial the wrong people all the time."

Heather took the pillow off her face and sat up. "Of course *you* do, Silver. But . . . yeeeah. Maybe he'll think it's a mistake and not even wonder about it. He'll probably just text me like always."

"Maybe. Let's watch TV and forget about it," I said. "Unless you really want to call him and not hang up this time."

Heather shook her head. "No, thanks. I'll pass."

She got up and grabbed the TV remote. She turned on our fave channel and sat cross-legged next to me. I leaned back against her headboard, relaxing. So she might not have talked to Troy, but at least she'd called him. Sort of.

Buzz!

Heather and I both jumped as her phone lit up between us.

"It's Troy!" Heather screeched, looking at the screen. "Omigod! What should I do? I can't answer it!"

"You have to! Or it'll look like you did call him and chicken out. Just answer it and be cool."

Heather stared at the phone for another second before she grabbed it and answered.

"Hey, Troy," she said, her voice a little higher than usual. She listened for a few seconds, then laughed.

"I was such a dork," she said. "I started to call you and dropped my phone."

Good line, I thought. Heather could totally do this.

I wanted to give her some privacy while she was on the phone. I motioned toward her laptop.

"Can I check my e-mail?" I mouthed.

Heather nodded, not even listening to me. She was too distracted.

I picked up her laptop and sat in the chair by the sliding glass door. I opened it and pulled up Hotmail.

Weird. My e-mail address was already typed into the box. No password, but I had no idea why my e-mail address would be in the box.

Heather doesn't use Hotmail, duh, I reminded myself. My address was probably still there from the last time I'd checked my e-mail on Heather's computer, days ago. In my rush to get out of Canterwood, I'd forgotten my own laptop, and Heather had said I could use hers if I needed to.

I started to type in my password.

"I've gotta run, Troy, talk to you later," Heather said quickly. She tossed down the phone, ran across the room, and snatched the laptop from me.

"Hey!" I said. "What're you doing?"

"Excuse me," she said. "What are *you* doing?"

"Checking my e-mail," I said.

Heather closed the laptop. "So you just take someone's laptop and use it?"

"I asked you! You were on the phone and I whispered if I could use your computer. You nodded, so I took that as the universal gesture of 'okay.'"

Heather's shoulders relaxed. "Sorry," she muttered. "You did ask. I just was so into my talk with Troy, I forgot I said yes. Here." She started to hand it back to me.

"Never mind," I said. "We're watching TV. I'll check it later, *after* I'm sure that you heard me ask you."

Heather smiled. "Okay. Deal. I'm going to ask Helen for a snack. Be right back."

Settling back against a couple of fluffy pillows, I shook my head. I couldn't figure her out sometimes. I thought we were past Heather thinking I'd snoop through her personal stuff on her laptop. And it wasn't even like I'd try to sneak away with it, lock my guest-room door, and use it. I was checking my e-mail right in front of her.

Heather walked back with a tray of food and closed the door with her foot. "TV time," she said.

"Most def."

And minutes later I'd forgotten about the weirdness over the laptop and we were laughing at the ridiculous antics of the latest cast of *Our World: NYC*.

20

GET YOUR GAME FACE ON

IT WAS BARELY DAWN ON FRIDAY MORNING when Heather and I stood near the front door, pulling on our riding boots.

"I'm so ready to practice," I said. I was surprisingly awake this early in the morning, but the vanilla cappuccino Helen had made me earlier *might* have had something to do with it.

"Me too," Heather said. We were both in black breeches and long-sleeve shirts. My cranberry-colored shirt was waffle knit and Heather's hunter green v-neck looked sophisticated with her breeches.

"Heather?"

I wanted to hurry into the hallway the second I heard Mr. Fox's voice.

"Yes, Dad?" Heather called.

"What's your plan for today's session?" he asked, striding into the room.

He held a steaming mug of coffee in one hand and a copy of *The Wall Street Journal* in the other.

"We're going to work on everything," Heather said, picking up her helmet from the floor. "Flatwork and jumping. We're doing posture exercises, too, and some new techniques I read about—almost like yoga in the saddle."

Mr. Fox nodded, his dark eyes on Heather's face. "That sounds like a solid plan. I want you to call me if you have any trouble finding a space to practice and I'll phone Pam immediately."

"I will," Heather said.

Mr. Fox sipped his coffee and turned, leaving the foyer.

"What would he do?" I whispered. "Have Pam throw riders out of the arena?"

"He'd try," Heather said. "But Pam's like Mr. Conner. She wouldn't put up with that. She'd tell him no way."

I picked up my own helmet and we headed for the car. I couldn't wait to get on horseback. I felt more at home in the saddle than I did at the Foxes' penthouse. And! A chill ran down my arms. Only two more days till I'd be riding *my* horse. I pictured Charm's face as we walked down the hallway. I couldn't wait to hug him and start training together for the schooling show.

More than half an hour later Heather and I walked down Chesterfield's aisle. We tacked up Limitless and Cora and led them toward the indoor arena. It was empty.

"Guess no one else is as crazy as we are to ride this early," I joked.

"Very true," Heather said.

We did a standard warm-up—walking, trotting, and cantering the horses so they wouldn't be stiff when we started a serious workout.

"Want to split up for a while and work on our own issues, then jump?" Heather asked.

"Sounds good," I said.

Heather rode Cora to the right end of the arena, and Limitless and I took the left. I started working him through spirals, paying attention to my hand and leg cues as I took him through the exercise. After a few spirals, we worked through circles, and then I stopped him. I dropped the reins around his neck and raised my arms out to my sides. I twisted a few times in the saddle and felt my back muscles loosen. I leaned down

and touched my toes, then straightened. I ran through a few more posture exercises before Heather rode Cora over to me.

"I think we've got flatwork down," she said. "If you're ready to stop and jump."

I glanced at the round wall clock. We'd been practicing for an hour but it felt as if I'd only been riding for a few minutes.

"I'm always ready to jump," I said.

There were a few portable jumps folded up along the wall. Heather and I dismounted and ground-tied the horses. Limitless cocked a back hoof and seemed glad for a break. I smiled as I walked away from him to help Heather set up the jumps. He was a good horse—I'd definitely miss him when I went back to Canterwood.

Together Heather and I set up five verticals of varying height. It was a simple course, but we'd run through it a couple of times.

"You can go first if you want," I said.

"Okay," Heather said. She heeled Cora into a trot and didn't waste any time guiding her toward the first jump. The mare leaped over the vertical. I loved how she landed without jarring her rider.

The next vertical was only a few strides away, and,

like the jump before it, Cora took it without hesitation. Heather had no trouble over the next three jumps. She rode Cora back to me with a smile.

"I don't even have to say it," I said. "That was amazing. Maybe you should steal Cora and take her back to Canterwood. You guys make a great team."

Heather laughed. "I'm sure Aristocrat wouldn't mind a break from a few practices."

"Probably not. I know Charm would sooo much rather spend time eating than practicing some days."

I gathered the reins and sat deep in the saddle. My turn.

Like Heather I didn't feel the need to circle Limitless before taking the first jump. We were ready, and I had jumped him before.

His canter was smooth and even as we moved forward. We reached the first jump and Limitless pushed up off the ground at the right second. The first jump wasn't too high, so he didn't need to expend much effort to clear it. Strides later the second vertical was in front of us. It was only a couple of inches higher—Limitless didn't even seem to notice. He soared over the red-and-white poles.

He snorted when he landed and we cantered toward the third vertical. I rocked in the saddle to his canter and rose into the two-point position at the right time. Limitless cleared the jump as if it were inches off the ground, and his hooves didn't even come close to touching the rail.

We took the fourth jump as if it wasn't even there and I let him out a notch for the final vertical. His canter quickened and he gathered his forelegs under his body as he launched into the air and over the rails. I grinned when he landed and cantered away from the jumps. Patting his neck, I rode him back to Heather.

"That was good," Heather said. "But wipe the grin off your face. We're not even close to being done."

"Yes, Mr. Conner," I said. I saluted her and she rolled her eyes.

"For that we're doing the next round without stirrups," Heather said sweetly.

Now it was my turn to make a face. But we were doing what we had to so we'd be as prepared as possible for the schooling show. And if riding without stirrups was what it took, I was game.

21

SHEER BLISS

"SILVER! SIIILVER."

I woke up to Heather shaking my arm.

"What?" I asked, looking at the clock. It was barely eight. "It's Saturday. We can sleep in a little, can't we?"

"Nooo," Heather said. "Not unless you want to miss our spa appointments."

That made me sit up.

"Spa appointments? Really?"

Heather grabbed my hand and yanked me out of bed, shoving me toward my closet.

"Really. Massages, facials, hot towels—all the good stuff. Dress in comfy clothes and meet me in the breakfast nook. We'll eat, and then we have to go."

Heather disappeared and I closed the door so I could

get dressed. I pulled on yoga pants and a soft cotton T-shirt. I picked up a pair of flip-flops and carried them into the bathroom, where I combed my hair and brushed my teeth. Before meeting Heather I dropped my flip-flops by the front door.

Heather was seated at the breakfast table, and there was a spread of food already laid out like a buffet. Immediately I went for the waffles and doused two of them with powdered sugar, syrup, and fruit.

Heather filled her own plate with eggs, two pieces of bacon, and French toast.

I almost inhaled my breakfast—I wanted to get out of there and go to the spa.

"I've *never* been to a spa, ever," I said. "Do we get to wear robes and everything?"

Heather nodded, finishing the final bite of her eggs. "Yep. And they'll wrap your hair in a towel so it won't get in your face mask."

"I'm sooo excited! This is going to be awesome."

We finished breakfast and met Paul at the car. I almost couldn't buckle my seat belt—my fingers were shaky!

"Calm down," Heather said. "It's a spa. It's supposed to be *relaxing*?"

"But also awesome," I said.

After what felt like hours, but was really only a few minutes, Paul pulled up to a place called Bliss.

"This is it," Heather said.

We said bye to Paul and got out of the car. The spa's outside was *so* cute! The overhang was pale blue, and the lettering on the door was white. I followed Heather inside and smelled so many calming and amazing scents—lemon, eucalyptus, lavender, and a few others I didn't recognize.

A waterfall cascaded down the main wall, making a soothing noise. I'd been inside for only a few seconds and I felt so serene.

Heather and I walked up to the counter.

"Hi," Heather said to the receptionist. "We have appointments for Heather Fox and Sasha Silver."

"One moment, please," said the receptionist. She flipped through a pink-and-white date book, then nodded. "I see you're both having full treatments done today. You'll have a lovely time, and enjoy Bliss!"

"Thanks," we both said.

The woman handed us two plastic-sealed packages.

"Inside each package," she said, "is a robe, disposable bikini, and a pair of slippers. Please change into those and we'll get you started. The changing rooms are straight down this hallway."

Heather and I found two empty rooms, and when I slipped into my fluffy white robe, I wanted to snuggle my face into it.

So. Soft.

I slid my feet into the equally comfy terry-cloth flip-flops and walked out. Heather emerged a second later, and a woman with perfect skin—would mine look like that after the treatments?—met us with a smile.

"Hi," she said. "Let me take your clothes and hang them up. I'm Emily and I'll be making sure you get to all of your sessions on time today."

"I'm Sasha," I said.

Heather offered Emily a hand. "And I'm Heather."

"Well, Sasha and Heather," Emily said. "Let's get you to your first treatment. Please follow me."

Heather and I followed Emily down a white hallway with a thin pink stripe running along the center of the wall.

"I've been here a few times, so I picked out the best treatments," Heather said.

"That's cool," I said. "I wouldn't have had any clue what to get."

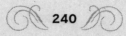

Emily led us to an open, airy room and handed us two towels.

"Wrap up your hair," she said. "Then have a seat. Your chairs are massage chairs that are heated. You'll be starting with a light exfoliation facial. Then you'll get a clarifying mask that will help with any blemishes or excess oil your face might have. I'll be back in about forty-five minutes to take you to your next session."

I climbed into my seat and settled back. Ooh, it *was* warm. I reached for the controller and played with the buttons. A nice rolling feeling started up and down my back, and I took a long breath as the massage chair got to work on the kinks in my back and neck.

"This is amazing," I said to Heather.

"Totally. And they haven't even started the facials yet."

Two women walked into the room and consulted clip-boards. They started mixing two batches of something peach colored in small bowls. They sat on rolling stools beside Heather and me. Everyone wore all white and just exuded calm—if that was possible. Barely audible clas-sical music played in the background, and I sank even deeper into my chair as my facialist put on gloves with tiny bumps on them and dipped her fingers into her mixing bowl. She smeared some of the mixture, which smelled like apricot, onto each of my cheeks, then put down the bowl.

I closed my eyes as she massaged the mixture into my face. I felt little exfoliating beads of something on my cheeks as she rubbed in circles.

It can't get any better than this, I thought. I kept my eyes closed and imagined how my skin would look when I left. It would be pretty and smooth when I went back to school.

After several minutes of the facialist rubbing the fruit-scented mix on my face, I felt a hot but not scalding washcloth. My facialist took her time wiping my face until all of the mixture was gone.

"Wow," I said, opening my eyes. "Thank you. That felt great."

She smiled at me. "You're welcome. I should have introduced myself before. I'm Anna."

"Sasha," I said.

Anna tossed the exfoliant mix and started pouring liquids and squeezing creams into another bowl. I touched a finger to my cheek.

Wow. So soft!

I looked over at Heather, who still had her eyes closed and her head resting back.

Anna came back and sat beside me. I closed my eyes as

she brushed a thin layer of something tingly on my face. It smelled so good—like mint.

"We're going to let that dry for about twenty minutes, then I'll peel it off," Anna said. "Relax in the meantime, and if you'd like, there are magazines in a basket beside you."

"Thanks," I said.

But I didn't feel like reading about the latest celebrity scandal. I wanted to sit back and enjoy every second of the spa environment.

It felt as if Anna came back almost a minute later, but she assured me it had been at least twenty. She peeled the mask from my face and squirted lotion into her hands.

"This moisturizer will make your skin even softer," she said. She reached over and held up a mirror. "Your face looks even more gorgeous."

I looked in the hand mirror, almost shocked by what I saw. The usual redness around my nose was gone, I couldn't see one blackhead, and my face just *looked* soft.

"Thank you so much!" I said. "My skin has never looked this good. Ever."

Anna smiled and took the mirror. I looked over, and Heather nodded at me.

"They're pretty good, huh?" she asked.

"So good," I said.

Emily walked into the room. "Did you enjoy your facials?" she asked.

"They were excellent, thank you," Heather answered, as I nodded.

"Wonderful! Up next is your body scrub."

Emily led us to a smaller room where everyone was separated by curtains. Men and women walked in and out of the curtained partitions and carried jars of different lotions and scrubs.

"Inside, hang up your robe on the hook and lie on the table," Emily said. "Someone will be with you right away. You're both getting the cream and sugar scrub, which will make you smell sweet and feel supersoft."

Emily pulled back a curtain and waved her hand, motioning me inside. The curtain swished behind me, and I took off my robe.

I got on the table, resting my head on the soft pillow.

"Hi, Sasha," a woman said, stepping beside me. She had silky black hair that was pulled back in a high ponytail. Her dark skin looked so smooth that I wondered if she got facials here every day. "I'm Keisha and I'm going to do your body scrub. You picked a great scrub—it's one of my favorites."

I smiled at her. "I came with my friend who comes here a lot, and she said it was awesome."

"You'll love it," Keisha said. She put a large bowl of scrub that smelled like just-out-of-the-oven vanilla cake at the end of the table. She took my hand and started rubbing the mixture on my hand and massaged it up to my elbow.

An hour later I was almost asleep as Keisha finished rubbing my foot.

"Was the scrub as good as your friend said it was?" Keisha asked.

"Better," I said. "That felt so good. Thank you."

Keisha smiled. "Walk straight forward to the showers. Rinse off the scrub, and then your guide will be here to take you to the next part of your treatment."

"Okay, thanks again." Keisha pulled back the curtain for me, and I walked to a glass door with SHOWERS etched on it. I pulled open the door and saw several showerheads. Some of the showers had sliding doors and others were public, like at a gym.

I was in a bikini, so I turned on one of the public showers and started rinsing off under the warm water. It was like Keisha had taken off a layer of my skin, but it didn't hurt. My elbows and knees had *never* been this smooth.

"Hey," Heather said. She walked over and turned on the shower next to me. She was covered in gritty scrub too. "Did you like it?"

"Like? Loved. I feel sooo relaxed."

Heather rinsed off her arms. "Me too. I think the mineral-water whirlpool is next. *That's* awesome."

"Then why are we in here?" I asked.

Heather nodded. "True."

We finished rinsing off and grabbed our robes. Emily, looking around, spotted us. Heather turned out to be right—the whirlpool was next. Heather and I got into the clear water and sat on padded ledges. The pool bubbled and the jets pushed the water against my freshly scrubbed skin. There was no one else in our whirlpool, so I stretched out my legs and ran my fingers through the water.

"So now I'm going to have to find a spa near Canterwood," I said. "I'm addicted."

Heather smiled. "I thought you would be. It's the most relaxing thing ever."

We fell into comfortable silence and enjoyed the whirl of the bubbles until Emily came to get us for our final treatment—lotion.

Keisha turned out to be the one who applied my coat of thick, creamy lotion to my skin. I had to sit in my robe for twenty minutes before she told me I could go change into my regular clothes.

I changed and found Heather in the hallway. She dug into her purse and pulled out a familiar credit card.

"Are you sure I can't pay for *some*thing?" I asked. "I have an emergency credit card."

"Stop it," Heather said. "My mom's paying for this. She owes us, so get over it."

I wanted to argue with her, but I knew I'd lose. "Okay. Thank you. Really."

"Just try to maintain that look when we get back to school," Heather said, eyeing me. "Or at least some of it."

I half-rolled my eyes.

Heather finished paying the bill and texted Paul to come get us.

"We'll grab lunch on the way home," Heather said. "Since it'll be your last lunch in the city, you can pick if you want."

I grinned. "Really? Then the Shake Shack for sure."

And as we walked outside to wait for Paul, I couldn't believe it was my last lunch in the city. At the beginning of the week I'd dreaded break—afraid that Heather and I would kill each other after spending a week together. But we'd become better friends than I'd thought possible, and I couldn't imagine a better break.

22

ALMOST EVERY DAY

ON SUNDAY MORNING I WOKE UP AND STARED at the ceiling. I'd spent my last night here, and tonight I'd be in my own bed in my dorm with Paige. I didn't want to think about that this early in the day, but I was going to be seeing her soon. And now I thought I was finally ready to talk. I didn't want life with my roommate and BFF to be uncomfortable, and I was sure Paige and I could work it out—I'd just needed time to see that.

Then I thought about the good things about going back to school. Like seeing Charm, prepping for the show, and figuring out my new friendship with the Trio.

I got out of bed and pulled a robe on over my T-shirt

and pajama pants. Heather's door was open and her room was empty. She had suitcases open, and a pile of clothes was on her already made bed.

I walked to the breakfast table and found her eating Greek yogurt with granola.

"Hey," I said.

"Hey," she said back. "I can't believe it's the last day of break. It went by so fast."

"I know." I put a plain bagel on my plate and reached for the strawberry-flavored cream cheese. "We're going to be so busy when we get back. I have all of my homework to do today and tonight."

Heather laughed. "Me too. It was ridiculous to assign homework over break. But whatev—that's Canterwood for you."

We ate our breakfast and I smiled at Helen when she started clearing our plates.

"Thank you for everything," I said to her. "I appreciate it."

Helen nodded. "Of course, Sasha. It was great to have you as a guest. I hope to see you again soon."

Heather stretched her arms toward the ceiling. "We need to start packing. Paul's picking us up in a couple of hours."

"Okay," I said. I noticed that the apartment was quiet except for the kitchen, where Helen was doing dishes. "Are your parents up yet?"

Heather pushed back her chair and got up. "They were up hours ago. They both left early this morning for a trip to Los Angeles."

"Did you get to say good-bye?" I asked. There was *no* way they'd just leave without—

"Oh, *they* said good-bye—in a sticky note on the counter," Heather said. "Good enough."

"Heather." I got up and followed her to her room. "I'm sorry."

"I'm not upset, really," Heather said. She walked into her closet. "They do this all the time. They just don't think to tell me when they're doing something because they're so used to me not being here. It was a big deal that they wrote a note, believe me."

"Still. Sorry," I said.

"Omigod!" Heather walked out of her closet, carrying an armload of clothes. "Stop! Seriously! Go pack or you'll go back to Canterwood without your stuff."

"Okay, okay." I looked at her for another second, and then left her room. She really *didn't* seem upset. And that made me sad, because it meant she was used to her parents

acting like that. I went into the bathroom first and gathered my shampoo, conditioner, body wash, and other toiletries. Before I put everything away, I washed my face and brushed my teeth. Then I put them in a Ziploc in case something leaked and put the bag in my suitcase.

Back in my room I pulled on jeans and a plain white T-shirt. It would be a comfy outfit for the ride back to school.

It didn't take me long to pack my clothes, since I hadn't brought too much. I had to squeeze in my new clothes, but I got the zipper to go all the way around the suitcase.

I checked the time on my phone—I'd made it with half an hour to spare. I noticed my text alert icon near my clock.

Paige, I thought. Since we were on our way to making up, I needed to at least read the text.

So glad we got 2 email so much over break. Rlly hope u show up @ the fountain.

What? Then I almost hyperventilated when I read the name.

Jacob.

My brain went into overdrive. I hadn't e-mailed him once over break! I'd barely checked my e-mail. Why would he write me and say he was glad we'd e-mailed when we hadn't? And what was he talking about, me meeting him? Had he meant to text someone else?

I sat at the end of the bed and stared at the phone. Minutes ticked by.

Then, in a rush, it all made sense.

The frequent IMs to "Julia" or "Alison."

The freaking out when I used her computer.

The error message when I tried to check my e-mail from my phone.

Heather Fox had hacked into my e-mail.

I ran out of my room and almost knocked over a table as I darted to her room.

"Were. You. On. My. E-mail?" I punctuated each word with force.

Heather looked up from her suitcase and her eyes met mine.

"Yes," she said. No hesitation, no lying. Just a simple yes that made the room spin.

My breath was ragged. "Did you e-mail Jacob?"

Heather nodded. "As you. Almost every day."

I stood, frozen, in her doorway. I couldn't formulate a sentence. I tried to breathe, but I couldn't do that either.

Then all of my strength came back. I stepped into Heather's room, slamming the door so hard behind me that her mirror shuddered.

23

UP TO YOU

"YOU SENT E-MAILS TO *JACOB*?!" I YELLED. I imagined everyone on every floor of the entire building heard me.

"Someone had to do something," Heather said, her tone calm. "You *like* like him. He's into you. You weren't doing anything about it, so I wanted to help."

I opened my mouth, stunned. It took me a long time before I could respond. "*Help?* You think sending e-mails as *me* to *him* helped?! What is wrong with you?"

"Sasha, I didn't tell him you hated him or that he dressed weird," Heather said. "I told him you liked him and missed him. And that's the truth."

"But it wasn't your truth to tell!" I couldn't stop yelling—my tone wouldn't lower.

Heather sat at the end of her bed. She didn't look sorry at all.

"Someone had to tell him. And I owed you."

"Owed me? For what?" I threw up a hand.

Heather held up her phone. "For what you did for Troy and me. I . . . wouldn't have texted him, let alone called him, if you hadn't pushed me."

Heather's voice was soft and she sounded so sincere. But that didn't matter right now.

"Okay, so you could have said 'Thank you, Sasha,' or bought me ice cream when we got back to school. Something—anything—but e-mailing Jacob. He's going to be waiting for me tomorrow at the fountain!"

Heather didn't say anything. She just watched me.

I fell into one of Heather's chairs and buried my face in my hands. "I have to go back to school tomorrow," I said. "And what am I supposed to do?"

I heard footsteps and felt papers placed on my lap. I looked down and saw that it was a printout of every e-mail between Jacob and "me."

"That," Heather said, "is up to you."

Jammed full of surprises!

LiP SMACKER.
LOUNGE

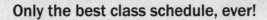